ABOUT THE AUTHOR

Dave Rigby lives in West Yorkshire and started writing shortly after he retired seven years ago.

SHORELINE is his second novel.
He published **DARKSTONE** in 2015.

SHORELINE

A HARRY VOS INVESTIGATION

DAVE RIGBY

Matador
9 Priory Business Park,
Wistow Road, Kibworth Beauchamp,
Leicestershire. LE8 0RX
Tel: 0116 279 2299
Email: books@troubador.co.uk
Web: www.troubador.co.uk/matador
Twitter: @matadorbooks

ISBN 978 1785891 380

British Library Cataloguing in Publication Data.
A catalogue record for this book is available from the British Library.

Printed and bound by CPI Group (UK) Ltd, Croydon, CR0 4YY
Typeset in 11pt Minion Pro by Troubador Publishing Ltd, Leicester, UK

Matador is an imprint of Troubador Publishing Ltd

SHORELINE

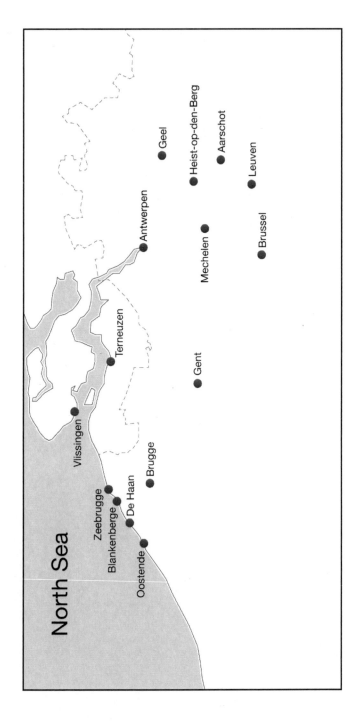

FLANDERS – BELGIUM

North Sea

Zeebrugge
Blankenberge
De Haan
Oostende
Vlissingen
Brugge
Terneuzen
Antwerpen
Gent
Mechelen
Geel
Heist-op-den-Berg
Aarschot
Leuven
Brussel

One

The man watched as the tram moved slowly along the coastal track, towards Oostende, as if struggling to push its way through the sea mist. He turned and limped through the sand dunes to the beach. It had been a favourite place of theirs. He walked to the water's edge and gazed at the ebb and flow, thinking of Margriet.

Through the mist he could see a shape being pushed up the beach by the waves. It was only when he drew nearer that he could see it was the body of a man. His mind flashed back to his father's body all those years ago and his first instinct was to turn and run. But he forced himself to look again, before stooping to try and drag the corpse away from the incoming tide. But it was heavy, the clothes waterlogged and he struggled to make progress.

He stood up, looking for help, scanning what little he could see of the beach. He was in luck. A tall, older woman in a long, old-fashioned raincoat was walking her dog towards him.

"I've just found this poor chap. Can you help me pull him up the beach? I don't want him to be washed away." He was breathing heavily and found it hard to talk.

"Yes, I could see you struggling with something but I didn't realise at first that it was a dead man. No doubt he's a dead weight too." The woman was clearly unperturbed by the body and spoke in a brisk, almost military manner. "Here, I'll grab him under the arm this side, you do the other." The dog sniffed around and then, losing interest, wandered off, its lead trailing in the wet sand.

Between them, they managed to drag the body a short distance away from the sea.

"I'd better call the police." The man pulled a mobile phone from his pocket. His hands were shaking and he had difficulty in punching in the three digits. "Damn, there's no signal. Do you have a phone?" The woman rummaged in her bag.

"I'm sorry, I seem to have left it in the apartment – how silly of me."

"Don't worry," he said, looking away from the beach. "There's a bar over the other side of those dunes. I'll try that. Are you OK to stay here and keep an eye on our friend?" He felt he was gradually regaining his composure.

"Well, he's not going anywhere, but I'll stay here and stand guard. I might as well have a coffee while I wait." She took off her small backpack and removed a silver flask.

"I'll be off then. I'll be as quick as I can." The man set off using his walking stick to try and propel himself along a little faster. When he reached the dunes, he looked back over his shoulder, but already the mist had enveloped the shoreline. The path through the dunes was clear enough. He tried his phone again, but there was still no signal. He felt the damp seeping through the lower part of his trousers as he pushed his way through the spiky marram grass, wet from the overnight rain. He kept wondering what had happened to the dead man. Numbness crept over him as he walked. It wasn't like the first time, after his father's car crash, when he'd been terrified.

Through the mist he saw coloured fairylights hanging lifelessly under the eaves of the single-storey Dune Bar. Two women were sitting at a white plastic table, drinking from small, blue cups and blowing cigarette smoke into the still air. He nodded to them and pushed open the door to the bar. The barman was hunched over the counter reading a newspaper, a glass by his side despite the early hour.

"Can I use your phone?" The question was blunt. "It's an emergency."

"Help yourself, mister," the barman said. "It's on the wall, in the corridor through there, just before you get to the toilets." He found the payphone and dialled 101.

"Hello. I've just found a body. My name? Vos, Harry Vos. No I'm just staying in town for a couple of days. What? Oh, 'The Canal'. No, not very original. What was I doing on the beach? Well I don't think I need a reason to be on a beach, but as it happens I was just having a walk. Listen, the body is on the beach just near where I'm phoning from – the Dune Bar, do you know it? Of course. There's a woman down there on the beach keeping an eye on things. No, I don't know her name. She was just out walking her dog. Yes he's definitely dead – a young black man. Pulse? No, I didn't check it, no need. Fifteen minutes. OK." Vos replaced the receiver and took a deep breath. At least his hands were no longer shaking. He returned to the bar.

"Did you get through OK?" the barman asked. Vos nodded. "Good. You want a drink? You look like you could do with one."

"No thanks, I have to meet the police."

He departed abruptly. He wanted to avoid the barman's inevitable questions and to get back to the beach as quickly as his leg would allow him. It ached more than usual on the return journey, but then it was always worse in the damp weather. The mist was still thick, but he managed to find his way back through the dunes and on to the shore. His trousers, soaked for a second time, clung to his lower legs.

As he headed towards the sound of the waves he tried make sure he was walking in a straight line, but without landmarks it was pure guesswork. He shouted for the woman. There was no reply. He shouted again – but there was just an empty silence. He wondered if he'd veered off track. But even if he had, surely she'd still be able to hear him.

He walked up and down the shoreline but there was no sign of the woman, her dog or the body. He was on his own. He listened to the waves on the wet sand and then heard a siren gradually getting louder. A patch of mist turned blue, the siren stopped and two uniformed men jumped out of a small Citroen.

"Are you Vos?"

"Yes."

"Where's this body then?" The voice betrayed no trace of concern. Vos played for time. Maybe he was mistaken about the location.

"Well it's a little hard to tell in this damn mist, but it's around here somewhere. We pulled him a little way up the beach, me and the woman."

"And I suppose the woman has disappeared as well, sir." It dawned on Vos that if he wasn't careful, he'd be seen as a police time-waster, a hoax caller.

"Look, I can't explain it. Let's have a look around." They traipsed up and down the shoreline to no avail. The mist gradually lifted. The beach was empty.

"I suppose the sea could have washed the body away," Vos said, increasingly desperate.

"And washed the woman away as well? I think we'd better go back to the station, sir, don't you?"

+ + +

It took Vos a long time and two phone calls to convince the police that he wasn't a complete idiot. His old boss at the factory had vouched for his sanity and his doctor had, reluctantly it seemed to Vos, confirmed this judgement.

When he asked the officer what they were going to do about investigating the case he looked at Vos witheringly.

"What case would that be, Mr Vos?"

As he left the police station, he could almost feel his tail between his legs. He got a taxi back to the Dune Bar where the barman was not surprised to see him.

"You'll have come back for that drink then."

Vos nodded absent-mindedly and muttered his thanks. "Brandy please. It's disappeared, the body that is."

The barman looked shocked.

"Oh, I'm sorry, I didn't tell you, did I?" Vos slowly explained the chain of events, stopping occasionally to sip his brandy. "It's all very strange, makes me think I was dreaming or hallucinating or something."

"Did you say this woman had a long raincoat on?"

The question came from behind him. Vos turned round. His questioner was a young man wearing a fluorescent top over a dark running vest and a pair of tight leggings.

"It's just that I saw a woman dressed like that when I was running on the beach earlier. Thought it was unusual – most of the dog walkers have those modern, expensive waterproof jackets. Dog was unusual as well. Irish wolfhound I think."

"Nice to know I wasn't making things up," Vos said, relieved. "Yes – the dog was different, sort of tall and thin."

"She called him Barto, or something like that. She had to call him to heel as I ran past."

"This is all really helpful. Let me jot it down before I forget." Vos pulled out a small red notebook and a black biro from his inside jacket pocket and scribbled a few notes.

"So, what are the police doing about this?" the barman asked as he topped up his own glass.

"No body, no evidence, no case was their view," Vos said.

"You going to turn private eye on this one, then?" the runner asked with a smile. Vos considered the irony of this.

"I might just do that," he replied, then turning to the barman, said, "Thanks for your help and for the drink. How much do I owe you?"

"Oh, don't worry about that – it's on the house. Where are you off to now?"

"Back to the hotel – The Canal – to dry out," Vos said, staring at his still-damp trousers.

"Well, mind how you go and good luck."

Vos decided against going straight back to the hotel. For the third time that morning, he walked through the dunes to the beach. The mist had cleared completely. The beach was empty and the tide was ebbing. He walked along the shoreline looking for anything which might help to explain what had happened to the body and the woman.

He turned it all over in his mind. It was unlikely that the body had been washed away, as the tide had still been coming in when the police had arrived. So it must have been removed either by boat or by a vehicle on the beach. He dismissed the sudden image he had of the woman carrying off the body, over her shoulder, to a waiting car. Still, he thought, she might have been in on it, whatever 'it' was. A boat seemed the most likely explanation, although the sea mist would have made a recovery job difficult.

He was about to turn away and walk back to his hotel, when something half-buried in the sand caught his eye and he stooped to pick it up. It was a bracelet or amulet of some kind, with distinctive, patterned markings and a few words engraved in a language he didn't recognise. Maybe it had been on the wrist of the young man and the sea had worked it loose. Vos did his best to recall the man's face, definitely African he thought, but not from the north. He felt he now had something to go on – a little tenuous perhaps, but better than the nothing he'd had a few minutes earlier.

+ + +

Back at the Hotel Canal, he changed out of his damp clothes and took a leisurely shower. He still had a day's holiday left and he'd almost forgotten that he was due to meet Monica that evening – their second date. It felt strange to be still dating at his age.

Dressed in jeans, a black and grey striped shirt and a dark fleece, he sat in his favourite position by the window, overlooking the canal. He indulged in a coffee and a cheese salad sandwich and glanced at the headlines in the Gazet Van Antwerpen.

But he couldn't concentrate on anything other than the body on the beach. Where had the poor man come from? Vos decided that if he was going to stand any chance of answering this question he'd need some expert help. He switched on his laptop and waited while the increasingly slow machine went through its preliminaries. He really should buy a new one. He decided to try one of the university websites and picked Antwerp Rubens, where he found a 'Department of Languages and Cultures of Africa' and a list of lecturers. It seemed as good a place to start as any. He made a note of the names and phone numbers of two of the academics and dialled the first number. It went straight to voicemail, with a message informing him that Mr Thijs was away on a study tour and wouldn't be returning until the summer. Alright for some, Vos thought.

A woman answered his second call and posing as an amateur anthropologist he explained briefly what he wanted to know. The woman said that Ms Verlinden was giving a lecture but would return his call when she returned to her office. Vos decided not to hold his breath waiting for the call.

+ + +

The *Leopold* eased its way into the old fishing harbour at Zeebrugge and docked at the quayside. Rodenbach climbed up the steel ladder and stood on the dockside cursing the day. What a disaster, and he was all too aware that it could get worse. Still he'd managed to put the fear of God into the woman and was convinced she wouldn't talk.

He knew he'd have to phone Hendrickx and give him a highly edited account of what had happened, but decided to put it off. He reflected bitterly that the worst part of the whole sorry mess was that he wouldn't get paid.

He unlocked the steel door to the dockside warehouse, went in, slammed the door behind him and made his way up the creaking wooden staircase to the first floor office. A young woman in a short skirt and heeled ankle boots filled a kettle, turned it on and spooned ground coffee into the inner chamber of a percolator that had seen better days.

"How was it, Leo?"

"Since you ask, Sabina, it was a fucking awful night! We lost one overboard. I mean we got the body back but it should never have happened. Daems has got to go. I don't know why I've hung on to him."

"Jesus, Leo, what do you mean you got the body back again? Where is it?" She stood staring at Rodenbach, open-mouthed.

"Relax, it's all under control."

Sabina looked unconvinced. She poured the boiling water into the percolator which commenced its routine of slightly disgusting sounds. She watched as her man sat down on a worn leather sofa and hauled his boots off.

"Those socks need changing, Leo – they stink to high heaven. Does Hendrickx know about the body?"

Rodenbach groaned, but didn't answer. He stretched out on the sofa and closed his eyes. He was back on the boat, him and Daems scanning the dark waters for the man overboard, straining to see anything through the thick sea mist. Daems claimed he'd only been defending himself, but that somehow the man had fallen over the rail. Having lost valuable minutes turning the boat, Rodenbach had known that their search would be pointless.

Rodenbach realised Sabina had asked him a question, but he'd been lost in his daydreams. She nudged him sharply in the ribs and he opened his eyes to see a mug of coffee in front of him.

"Not that you'll take a blind bit of notice of me, but you need to get this sorted out right away and you need to tell Hendrickx before somebody else does."

He knew she was right.

+ + +

The noise of the phone startled Vos. He must have dozed off in the warmth of the hotel room. It was a woman's voice.

"Mr Vos – hi, it's Katerine Verlinden from the university. You wanted to talk to me about an amulet of some kind, is that right?"

He tried to gather his thoughts – he really hadn't expected her to return his call.

"Oh, yes…er… that's correct. Thanks very much for calling me back. To tell you the truth I'm doing a bit of detective work on an amulet I found on the beach. It's a sort of hobby of mine. Would there be any chance of me coming to see someone in your department to try and track down the origin of this item? I could perhaps scan a picture of it across to you, but I always prefer doing things face to face if possible. What do you think?"

To his surprise, she agreed and they arranged to meet the following day. It was convenient for Vos, as he'd be able to call in to the university on his way home. The thought of home jogged his memory and he phoned his nephew Ryck.

"How's it going, Ryck? Good, no break-ins then! Excellent. Listen I'll be back tomorrow, probably around six. Could you put the heating on just to air the place a little? Many thanks. What's that? Grandma's not so good. OK, thanks, I'll give her a ring now."

Ryck kept an eye on Vos' house during his frequent absences and also helped out with the garden. If he was honest with himself, Vos had to admit that Ryck did the lion's share of the gardening.

Vos dialled his mother's number.

"Hello Mother, I hear from Ryck that you're not so good." She told him of her breathing problems which were getting worse. "Listen, I'll be back tomorrow. I'll call round about half six if that's OK. What…bingo? Oh, OK I'll make it eight. See you then. I've got a bit of a mystery to tell you about. No, Mother, it's nothing dangerous."

He changed his clothes again and brushed his teeth twice to be on the safe side. He wanted to be in peak condition for Monica. But wasn't he just kidding himself – overweight, limping, averse to buying new clothes – what did she see in him? Even though it was ten years since his wife's death, Vos still felt ambivalent about dating other women and none of his relationships had lasted. It wasn't that they'd had a perfect marriage, but he and Margriet had always felt comfortable together. He had to work so much harder at new relationships. Still, he'd only met Monica a few days ago. Maybe it was a bit too early to be so pessimistic.

A taxi dropped him off at the restaurant Vivaldi. The restaurant was mid-range Italian. He tried to avoid the more formal places, full of hovering waiters and menus he couldn't understand. Like an eager, but apprehensive teenager he checked his wallet for the condom. It was there, nestling between his credit card and his library card. He moved it to a less accessible part of his wallet, to avoid the risk of pulling it out inadvertently.

Monica was late. Vos hated waiting for things, but he tried not to show his frustration when she finally arrived.

"So sorry, Harry. My daughter called just before I was due to set off and…well you know what it's like." He had to admit – he did know what it was like. Not that phone calls with his daughter were conversations. They were more like monologues.

"That's OK, Monica, I was keeping this glass of excellent red wine company. Here let me pour you one." But she placed her hand over the wine glass just before he started pouring.

"Sorry, it's one of my no alcohol days. I'll just have a sparkling water thanks." Vos hoped the evening wasn't going to continue in the same vein.

But it did. Once they'd finished the meal, she told him it was a 'school night' and that she had to be up early in the morning for some business meeting in Brussels. He still hadn't worked out what she actually did. With a hug and a quick peck on the cheek, she was off in her shiny Mercedes. Well maybe next time, he thought ruefully, as he paid the bill.

Two

Vos slept through his alarm. When he finally surfaced, he swore and, in too much of a hurry, tripped and fell on his way to the bathroom. At least he fell on his good leg.

Having skipped breakfast, he took the Kusttram to Blankenberge for the start of his journey back to Antwerp. He pretended to read the paper during the journey but spent most of his time listening to the conversations of his fellow passengers. At one point he asked a young man if it was possible for him to swear a bit louder so that the whole carriage could get the full benefit of his erudition. The youth looked confused and annoyed in equal measure. He got up and stomped off down the carriage to continue his phone conversation uninterrupted. One or two passengers nodded their appreciation to Vos.

At Antwerp, he emerged from the depths of the station and marvelled at the cathedral-like building. It never failed to impress him. He jumped on to a number 12 tram which deposited him at the right part of the university campus. His own secondary education had been abruptly interrupted and he'd never had the chance to go to university himself. Although he knew it was irrational, he'd always felt slightly in awe of graduates. At the reception desk he asked for Ms Verlinden and was directed outside to a pleasantly landscaped area. The woman sitting on one of the ornately carved wooden benches beckoned him over. She stood, smiled and shook his hand with a firm grip.

"Hi – Mr Vos?" He nodded. "I thought as the weather was good we could sit and talk out here. Rooms are always difficult to get here, especially as our business is unofficial." Another smile, which was almost conspiratorial. He was warming to this woman. She looked a few years younger than him, medium height, dark hair, smartly dressed. There was something else that he couldn't quite put his finger on. It was only later he realised that she looked like a slightly taller version of his late wife.

"That's fine." Vos said. "I'm really pleased you could afford the time to see me. I mean it's something of a wild goose chase I'm on. Perhaps I'd better fill you in."

He told her the full story of what had happened the previous day and showed her the amulet. She was immediately interested, handling it carefully and examining the inscription.

"Well, I can't be certain, but I think this is from the Democratic Republic of the Congo. It's malachite, a form of copper. There's a lot of it mined in Katanga Province. Sorry, that won't mean much to you. We do a lot of work on artefacts which originate in the DRC – the old colonial links of course."

"And have you any idea what the inscription says?"

"I'm not sure. It's a version of Swahili, but I can't quite follow it all. I think it might be something to keep the traveller safe – a bit like a St Christopher medal. Unfortunately it doesn't seem to have worked. At a guess I'd say your unfortunate man was being smuggled or trafficked into the country – a long journey which he was prevented from completing. What do the police say?"

Vos explained their lack of interest in the case.

"So, are you some sort of private investigator?"

He rubbed his chin and then pinched the bridge of his nose, his usual delaying tactic. "You could say that. Between you and me, I'm an unlicensed amateur who gets paid only in cash – not that there's anyone to pay me for this job. I'm doing it for my own interest and for the dead man. The PI work started, would you believe, when my sister asked me to track down my brother-in-law who'd buggered off. That was another job without pay. But I've got a reasonable pension, so I don't always have to take paid work." He thought he was saying too much, but she seemed interested, and asked him whether he'd managed to track down his brother-in law.

"Yes, I found him, in a bar, which was no surprise, but it was two hundred kilometres from his home. My sister didn't really want him back, just wanted maintenance for herself and her son Ryck. I had the right form in my pocket and got him to sign it over a glass of Leffe. I was quite pleased with myself. That was about five years ago. Since then I've done a few more disappearances, with mixed results, a couple of debt recoveries, lost dogs, and a stolen car where the client, if I can call him that, didn't want the police involved."

"It sounds like you lead a varied and interesting life." Vos couldn't tell whether she really meant this or whether she was gently making fun of him. She continued. "So, is there anything more I can do to help?"

"Oh, I hadn't really thought that far. Um...well, it would be really useful to know where the amulet originated, I mean, which part of the DRC. I don't know whether it's likely, but if you were able to pinpoint a specific area, it could help us to try and track down the family of the dead man. I'm probably being hopelessly unrealistic, but I want to try and do something."

"It's too early to tell, but we can trace the origins of some of these artefacts to very specific locations, so you never know, we might strike lucky."

He was in two minds whether to leave the amulet with her. After all it was the only bit of evidence he had. Still, without it she'd be able to make little progress. It was her suggestion that they meet again, so she could hand the amulet back and update him on progress. He told her he'd look forward to it.

On the walk back to the station, he stopped at a van selling chips. His doctor had told him he needed to lose weight and he was supposed to be on a diet. He convinced himself that this was an exceptional situation because he was celebrating both his progress on the case and his meeting with an attractive woman. He resisted the temptation to cover the chips in mayonnaise and took great delight in eating them very slowly as he made his way to the station, keeping his guilt at bay.

+ + +

A troupe of dancers enlivened the station concourse, their bright costumes contrasting with the sober dress of commuters, the lively sounds of the accordions reverberating around the cavernous space. Vos stood for a while tapping his feet and thinking of his own dancing days. Ever since the accident he'd found his movements lacked a certain rhythm. He tore himself away from the carnival atmosphere and made his way to the train. He dozed on the journey back home and his nephew Ryck picked him up in the car at Heist-op-den-Berg station.

Vos considered himself to be a relative newcomer in Heist, a straggling settlement, sort of all over the place and nowhere at the same time. He still thought of himself as an Antwerp man, even though he hadn't lived there since the age of sixteen. His house was about a mile from the train station, a long, low, single-storey home with an uneven, red pantile roof. It was surrounded by a large garden which was mainly dedicated to the growing of vegetables. At the back of the house there was a well-trimmed lawn which boasted a sun lounger that got very little use and a working well that had its own tiny pantile roof. Beyond the lawn was a large shed.

Ryck, who still lived with his mother, parked up on the concrete driveway, exchanged Vos' car for his own scooter and rode home. Vos poured himself a beer and settled into his armchair. The house was pleasantly warm. He was about to reach for the TV remote when his phone rang.

"Yes?" Vos responded abruptly. He heard a woman's voice, one that he couldn't place, but which was vaguely familiar.

"Mr Vos, I'm sorry to have to call you. My name is Simone Josse. I'm the woman who was on the beach, you know, near De Haan, with the body and the dog." She paused. Vos was taken aback and asked how she'd managed to track him down.

"Ah well it's a bit of a story. You remember you said you were going to the bar to use their telephone? Well, I found the bar and the proprietor told me you were staying at the Hotel Canal. You see I needed to find you. At the hotel, they gave me your telephone number." Vos said he was surprised they'd released that information.

"So was I, Mr Vos, but I can be very persuasive. I managed to convince them that it was an emergency – which I suppose it is really." She paused again briefly. "I'll come to the point. Just after you left, an absolutely awful man arrived in one of those four wheel drive vehicles – you know the kind. He'd been driving along the shoreline and had spotted me and of course the body of the man. He seemed quite upset at first and told me how he'd been searching for his crewman. He explained that the man had fallen overboard, couldn't swim and had been washed away from the boat. He must have been brought ashore by the incoming tide." Vos wondered where this story was leading. Simone continued talking.

"The 4x4 driver said he'd take the body away in his vehicle and report the accident to the authorities. When I told him that the police were already on their way, his manner changed abruptly. He became very hostile and more or less abducted me, along with the body."

Vos was having difficulty taking Simone's story in. Because

she hadn't been there when he'd returned to the beach, he'd half-forgotten about her and hadn't even considered tracking her down. Well, she was obviously more dogged than he was. He told her what had happened when he'd returned to the beach, about the police and their lack of interest in the body.

"So, there's nothing happening," Simone said. "Perhaps we could meet up to decide what, if anything, we should do next."

"Where are you now?" Vos asked. "Are you still on the coast?"

"No, no, I was only there for a couple of days. I'm back home now. I live near Geel. And you?" Vos told her he was only just down the road at Heist. "Well, well, what a coincidence. Look, I'd really like to meet up and talk it all through. Would that be possible? Perhaps I could come to your house?"

They agreed to meet at eleven the following morning.

Vos picked up his beer glass and realised it was empty. He fetched a second bottle from the fridge and refilled the glass. He felt relieved that the body, the woman and the dog all really existed. Simone Josse had sounded interested in finding out more although, he had to admit, she'd sounded worried as well – not shit-scared as Ryck would have put it, but certainly wary. Her description of the man with the 4x4 confirmed Vos' own worries – those he'd been trying to bury since his conversation with Katerine – that something criminal had been going on. His hunch was that it had to be smuggling-related, either drugs or people – or possibly both. He knew he'd need to be cautious, but caution had never been a strong suit of his.

As he settled into his chair once again, he remembered about his mother. He didn't feel like going anywhere. The last two days had taken it out of him and he just wanted to sit in front of the TV. But he knew that wouldn't be possible. Reluctantly he hauled himself out of the comfort of his well-padded chair, put on his coat and scarf and grabbed his walking stick.

His mother lived only ten minutes walk away, so she was near but not too near. He got on well enough with her, but they always ended up arguing if they spent too long together. There'd been several years after his father's death when she'd been permanently grief-stricken, tearful and depressed, but then she'd gradually picked up the pieces and started to live again. He didn't know what had brought about this change.

There were still traces of a brief snow flurry on the pavement but they were rapidly melting and, even in the streetlight, he could see that buds were beginning to show on the hawthorn hedges. He enjoyed the short walk. An outside light illuminated his way up the path to his mother's front door, where he knocked and waited. She had offered him a key, after his father's death, but he'd felt it would have been a bit of an intrusion to take it. She still had all her marbles. If she started to lose her memory, then a key would become a necessity.

"Did you win anything, Mother?"

"Of course I did, I always win. Why do you think I go?"

"Well, I thought perhaps you might meet up with someone special there."

She looked at him as if he was a small boy again, some boundary he'd crossed. But her look gradually softened.

"Don't just stand there, Harry, come on in and pour the drinks." She'd always been a beer drinker. He opened the beer cupboard and selected a cherry beer for her and a gueuze for himself. They sat opposite each other.

"How are you then, Mum? Ryck said you weren't so good."

"That boy talks too much."

"He's hardly a boy and he's only got your interests at heart. Do you need to change your inhaler? Have you seen the doctor?"

"Too many questions, Harry! No, I'm just a bit tired and when I get tired I get a bit puffy. It's nothing. It'll pass. Have you seen your brother recently? He seems to be going through one of his quiet phases."

"I was up at the bungalow a couple of weeks ago. Pieter seemed OK, a bit withdrawn. There seemed to be something on his mind but he wouldn't tell me what it was. I'll try and get up there again soon but I've got a little investigation on at the moment which might take up some time."

"Oh – so what have you been up to on the coast?"

Vos had already decided not to tell his mother about the body. There was no need to worry her unnecessarily. Instead, he told her about the amulet, the beach walks, the hotel and Monica. At the mention of a woman's name, his mother was suddenly all ears.

"Is she, you know, a bit more than short term?"

"Oh, so it's OK for you to ask me personal questions, but I'm banned from asking you. Well if you must know I don't hold out much hope with her. She's younger than me, got some high-flying job, but I think she's just after a good dinner now and then."

"What do you expect if you tangle with young professional women?"

"She's not that much younger than me and I thought you always said I should try and improve myself."

They talked for a little longer, until their glasses were empty. He kissed her on the forehead and let himself out. His return walk was illuminated by a crescent moon. He followed the movements of a bat as it zig-zagged across the lane. He thought about Katerine Verlinden and decided he'd ask her out to dinner, the next time they met.

Three

Up late the following morning, Vos stood in the shower and felt the hot water pounding against his skin. He could hear the muffled sounds of the news headlines on the radio. He was a radio addict, had the thing on most of the day, in the house, in the car, in the shed.

He dried himself with a huge, fluffy, white towel and then put on a dressing gown and slippers. Breakfast was coffee and scrambled eggs with the newspaper propped up against the coffee pot, the radio playing a series of pieces by Cesar Franck. He stopped reading and started to scribble down rough notes for his plan of attack on the garden. He found he could no longer manage the digging and he'd borrowed a rotovator from a neighbour. He jotted down a list of vegetables, where and when they'd be planted. Chewing on the end of his pen and lost in his plan, he was at first surprised by the sound of the doorbell. The clock on the mantelpiece said eleven and he realised Simone Josse was exactly on time.

He answered the door with his dressing gown pulled tightly around him. The woman was wearing the same long raincoat she'd had on when they'd first met on the beach. She didn't seem to notice that he hadn't got round to dressing.

"Welcome, come on in Simone. Er, if you'll excuse me for a few minutes I'll just throw some clothes on. Make yourself comfortable – there's some coffee in the pot."

He returned to the kitchen a few minutes later, dressed for the day, and they sat at the large pine table.

"Well, Mr Vos, I suppose I ought to tell you what happened in a bit more detail. I didn't have chance to say much on the phone. I've been thinking about the young man we found on the beach. I'm fairly sure he must have been from West Africa, but I couldn't say which specific country."

"What makes you think that?" Vos asked, trying to keep a sudden shakiness out of his voice. Talking about the dead man was more difficult than he'd thought it would be.

"Are you alright, Mr Vos? You sound a little upset." Vos waived his hand to indicate she should continue. "Well, as I said, I can't be certain, but I lived in the old Belgian Congo for many years and you get to recognise these things, facial characteristics I mean. It became almost instinctive for me. Anyway, enough of my speculations! Let me give you a little more detail about what happened on the beach. As I told you on the phone, the man was driving his 4x4 down the shoreline, half in and half out of the water. When he saw me and the body of the man he stopped abruptly and got out of the vehicle, looking relieved. He said he'd been searching for the body of his crewman, who'd been lost overboard. When he started to pull the body towards the 4x4, I told him the police were on their way and that perhaps he should wait until they arrived.

Sorry – I know I've told you that part of the story already. But anyway, it was as if a switch had been thrown inside the man's head. One minute he'd been full of concern and the next he was threatening me. I didn't know what was happening. He demanded some kind of ID. Luckily I had my driving licence in my bag and gave it to him. He read out my name and address and told me never to forget that he now knew where I lived. Then for good measure he photographed me with his phone, made it very clear that I should keep my mouth firmly shut and reminded me that I'd seen nothing. He bundled the body very roughly into the back of the vehicle and covered it with an old blanket, then forced me and Barto into the back seats and we drove off into the mist."

"Barto?" Vos queried.

"Yes, sorry, he's my dog, the Irish wolfhound you saw. I'm not a woman who's easily scared, but I have to say, the threats this man made are a bit of a worry. He's a big man, barrel-chested and very pugnacious. I didn't take to him at all. He obviously saw me as trouble. I'm surprised he didn't play it all very low key, you know, lost the man overboard, great shame, need to take the body with me and go to the authorities to sort out all the formalities – that kind of approach. But, oh no, he went at it like a bull at a gate. Come to think of it, he was a bit like a bull. After a few kilometres, he pulled up, and told me to get out of the car. He warned me again not to say anything to anyone under any circumstances. Luckily, I hadn't told him anything about you." She took a sip of her rapidly cooling coffee and asked if she could take a biscuit.

"Of course, help yourself." Vos took one himself. "Look, now that there are two of us who witnessed the body, perhaps we should go to the police. They might take us more seriously." Simone immediately looked apprehensive.

"Oh, no, I don't think so. I saw the man's face, heard him speak those words. I don't think he'd hesitate for a minute to come after me, if he suspected the police were involved. Subtlety is never a strongpoint with men like that. I'm sorry, Mr Voss, if this compromises you."

Vos said he didn't feel at all compromised, but he did share her worries about the man in the 4x4.

"Look," he continued. "I haven't had chance to tell you yet, but I went back to the beach after the police released me and I found an amulet, a sort of bracelet in the sand." He explained how he'd decided to see what he could find out about the amulet, the only clue he had. He told her about his discussion with the university lecturer and the enquiries she was making. "How would you feel about working together to find out more about what happened?" he asked. The idea had only just come into his mind. "We'd keep a low profile of course."

"Well, as long as we're very careful, I think that might be possible," Simone said. "I may be paranoid, but I think I might have been followed this morning, not all the way here obviously, but for the first twenty kilometres or so. Whoever it was, I threw him off at a level crossing, just managed to get through while he was left stuck at the barrier. So maybe that awful man is keeping track of my movements for a while."

Vos didn't know what to make of this. It seemed far-fetched. Was it just paranoia? On the other hand, she didn't seem like someone who would panic easily.

"Let's wait until I get some detail on the amulet and maybe we'll be able to use that to help us track down the identity of our man. You mentioned your time in the Congo. Do you still have contacts there?"

"Unfortunately I've lost touch with most of the people I knew when I lived there." She hesitated before continuing. "I probably shouldn't tell you this but you seem like a man I can trust. I do have contacts in the DRC through the, er…let's call it research, I carry out. It's rather sensitive so I can't say much about it just now. But it's another reason why it wouldn't be a good thing for me to get tangled up with the police."

Vos began to realise that he shouldn't underestimate this woman.

+ + +

The soil was heavy and the rotovator seemed to resent the task of breaking up the clods of earth. Vos struggled to control the machine as it bucked and heaved across the uneven ground. It

was still much quicker than the hand-digging of old, but he had
to watch his back and try to avoid too many jerking movements.
He wore an old stained boiler suit which he'd inherited from his
father, wellington boots and a flat cap. He waded through the
sticky morass, stopping periodically to scrape the mud off his
boots.

He turned the machine round at the top of the row and started
back towards the house. He wanted a coffee but told himself he
had to complete three more rows before allowing himself a break.

He hadn't had a case like this one before. After his success
in tracking down his brother-in-law, word had got round locally
about his skills. He enjoyed the variety of the work and his clients
were happy to pay him in cash, half up front and the rest on
completion.

This job was different. He assumed the man on the beach
probably hadn't died from natural causes and that made the job
much riskier. But that didn't stop him wanting to pursue it.

"Hi Harry!" In his day-dreaming Vos hadn't noticed his
nephew's arrival. "You want a hand?"

Vos decided that was exactly what he wanted – after they'd had
a coffee. His resolve to complete three further rows, before taking
a break, vanished into the slowly warming spring air. His boots
were caked in thick, heavy soil and he left them by the wooden
boot remover at the back door and walked into the kitchen in his
thick grey socks. Ryck followed him in his long, narrow, highly-
polished shoes, the sort of footwear that Vos wouldn't be seen
dead in. He made the coffee and they sat at the kitchen table, Ryck
helping himself to the packet of chocolate biscuits, Vos trying to
restrain himself.

"Do you know about Wouters?" Ryck seemed a little
embarrassed asking the question.

"Who?"

"Jan Wouters, he's a friend of Grandma's." Ryck lingered on

the word 'friend'. Vos' expression made it clear to Ryck that he'd never heard of the man. "It's a little difficult, but the word is, he's sort of going out with Grandma."

Vos stared at his nephew. What was his mother doing going out with anybody at her age? He tried to remain calm and focused.

"Who is this guy?" he asked.

Ryck explained that he lived not far away in Aarschot, had his own car, seemed quite well off and had something of a reputation as a ballroom dancer.

"Have you got an address?" Vos asked. Ryck said he hadn't, but he could easily find out. "Thanks, Ryck. That would be helpful. I need to check this man out." Vos tried, with difficulty, to push the subject to the back of his mind. "By the way, how long have you got for the garden?"

"A good couple of hours – I should be able to finish the patch off, save your legs and your back. I'll get cracking when I've finished this," he said, holding up his mug.

"Excellent. Thanks again." Vos wondered what he would say when he caught up with Wouters.

1968

"Get a move on Harry or you'll be late!" Mother stands over me making sure I've packed all my gear into my haversack.

It takes me less than quarter of an hour to cycle to the club. On the way there I'm Eddie Merckx, my cycling hero, head down, legs pumping, yellow jersey mine for the taking.

With the boxing gloves on, I always feel like a different person. Out goes the scrawny young lad and in comes someone to be wary of. I used to be small for my age, a target for the headcases at school, but the boxing has changed all that. And I've grown. The bullies leave me alone now. Coach used to be a professional in his day, but people say the drink ruined his career. Then he gave up the bottle and joined some church – got religion. He spends most of his time at the gym now, coaching the local lads. He says he has high hopes for me. I don't know about that. Perhaps he's just kidding me on, but my right jab is pretty good and I reckon I'm a quick learner. Coach says I need more control. I have to admit I've lost it a couple of times and he's had to pull me away from my opponent.

The training goes well and there's talk of some Antwerp contest. Coach says he'll put my name down for it. I think about this as I cycle home along the dockside. I'm not supposed to go this way – too many roughnecks there, my dad says. I'm not really concentrating and suddenly there's this big lad who I half-recognise, in the middle of the road, forcing me to stop. His mate is standing to one side sniggering. The big lad tells me he's got a knife in his pocket and demands money. Of course I haven't got any. I never have any – spend my pocket money as soon as I get it. I put the bike down on the ground and search my pockets, playing for time. He glances warily around and tells me to hurry up. He says something insulting about Pieter, my brother who's handicapped and I see red. I'm very protective about him – maybe over-protective. I let fly with my right which catches the big lad full on the jaw. He wasn't expecting anything. He falls heavily to the ground, his head hitting the cobbles hard. There's blood and I panic, get on the bike and career off down the street. I turn my head and see the other lad standing rooted to the spot.

Minutes later, the sound of a siren floats across the water. How can they know already? I turn around and cycle back to where the big lad is still lying on the ground. At first the police don't believe my story – the victim's too big surely. I don't tell them about the insult to my brother. I have a feeling that if I tell them it might save me, but somehow I can't. They put me in the back of a blue van and I sit on the floor and try to avoid sliding around at every corner.

Even in court I don't tell them what was said. There's a witness who says he saw everything from his bedroom window, two boys having a conversation and then without warning one of them lashes out unprovoked. But he couldn't have heard anything that was said. The prosecution tells the court I'm out of control and a danger to others. I need to be taught some discipline. I'm sentenced to eighteen months inside.

Four

"You're fucking joking!" Sabina couldn't believe what Rodenbach had just told her. "How do you mean the body is still on the boat? Whereabouts on the boat? What about the police?"

"Calm down, Sabina. It's all under control. The body's in the fish freezer. There's no reason why the police or anyone else should go snooping around the boat. We're properly licensed, our mooring fees are up to date, we have a very low profile. Why would anyone be checking up on us? We'll get rid of the body tonight, so there's nothing to worry about. Come back to bed. I'm getting cold in here."

But she continued to gaze out of the window, across the rooftops of the sheds and warehouses, wondering why she put up with Rodenbach. Sure, he was good in bed, bought her presents and took her dancing but he was basically unreliable. He'd get caught one day and she didn't want to go down with him. She noticed a man staring across at her. He was standing on a wooden balcony, less than ten metres away, holding a half-full glass of beer and smoking a cheroot. She stood naked at the window watching him watching her. In the end he turned away. She smiled and returned to bed.

+ + +

Rodenbach reversed the *Leopold* away from the quayside and allowed the vessel to drift slowly for a few moments, as he scanned the harbour area. He saw nothing unusual. The boat moved forward, gained speed and cleared the harbour wall out into the grey evening sea. There was a swell which suited him. He told Daems to take the wheel and he leant over the rail at the back of the boat and watched the lights of Zeebrugge as they slowly receded. After an hour he told Daems to cut the engine. The two of them opened the lid of the freezer and stared at the bodybag. They hauled it out of the freezer. The thick plastic of the body-bag was hard to grip as they stumbled their way forward. Rodenbach unzipped the bag and tried to avoid looking at the face of the dead man. He pushed heavy metal weights into the bag and re-zipped it.

"That should do. Now, grab the other end," he told Daems. They were just about to start lifting the bag when a small low-flying plane approached from the east. Rodenbach knew that customs used unmarked spotters. He quickly pulled a tarp over the bodybag and picked up a large rod, pretending to inspect the reel. He'd no idea how much they'd be able to see from the plane in the darkness but he was taking no chances. The aircraft roared past and its lights gradually disappeared into the gloom.

"Let's get this bloody job done and then we can go home." They attempted to lift the bag again, but struggled with the weight of it. Despite the cold night air, they sweated as they tried to lift the bag up high enough to topple it over the side of the boat. Eventually they succeeded. There was a loud splash and the bag disappeared from view. The pair of them collapsed onto the deck, breathing heavily. Daems pulled a bottle from his pocket, took a swig and handed it to his skipper. They sat and smoked for a long while, watching the stars emerging. The journey back to port was uneventful and they were relieved that there were no other vessels to be seen. Once they'd docked, Rodenbach walked to the tiny quayside bar. He ordered a cognac and declined the offer to join the card game. He felt relieved, but he still hadn't phoned Hendrickx.

+ + +

Vos phoned his son Eddie, in Antwerp to ask if he could stay the night.

"Sure, if you don't mind being woken at five in the morning by the terrible two. They're just as lively as ever." Eddie's twin sons didn't seem to need much sleep and they saw any overnight visitor as fair game for their early morning attacks.

"I'll cope! I'm going out for a meal with a woman friend from the university, but I shouldn't be late in. I'll bring my key, see you in the morning."

"So – mixing with uni people now are we? I hope she's nice." Vos ignored his son's comment and hung up.

The drive into Antwerp didn't take long in the mid-evening traffic. Katerine Verlinden had phoned him to say she had some news about the amulet. When he'd suggested meeting over dinner she'd sounded pleased. The small restaurant was in the Het Eilandje district in the old docks area, full of renovated warehouses and waterside bars – one of which was Eddie's. Vos left his car in a multi-storey close to his son's apartment and walked along the water's edge, worrying about his mother. He spotted Katerine outside the restaurant, talking animatedly into her mobile. She caught sight of him and rapidly finished the call. She seemed heated, ill at ease.

"Not bad news?" he asked, hoping that whatever it was, it wouldn't spoil their evening.

"Just my bloody ex who refuses to leave me alone! He's a control freak. I'm sorry, this isn't a very good way to start the evening. I'm really pleased to see you again, Harry." She sounded like she meant it. He was relieved.

They shook hands and went into the restaurant. The place was a little too formal for Vos' liking but the food was highly rated. At a table by the window, they ordered fish chowder starters, to be followed by beef stew cooked in Trappist beer. Katerine's mood rapidly lifted and Vos felt optimistic.

"So, what have you managed to find out, Katerine?"

"Hang on a minute, would you like another De Koninck before I go into detail?" Vos nodded and she beckoned the waiter to take the order. Vos was pleased about that, a woman who ordered the beers. "It's good news really," she continued. "I've managed to track down the broad area where the amulet originated. The malachite is from the copper belt in Katanga province. The inscription is in a language called Kingwana, which is also known as Copperbelt Swahili. But there are two words on the amulet in a local language which I haven't managed to identify yet. I took the liberty of speaking to a colleague of mine, a man called Jalloh at Brussels City University – I hope you don't mind. He's a specialist in tribal languages and I'm sure he'll be able to establish more precisely where the amulet came from. He's got a lot of contacts and not just academic ones. He'd be a good man for you to speak to. I have his contact details here." She handed Vos a business card. "I've worked with Jalloh a few times and he's a good guy, if a little brusque at times."

"You've made a lot of progress, Katerine. That's really helpful."

Vos took a sip of his beer and paused whilst the waiter placed a large white tureen and a ladle in the middle of the table. They helped themselves to soup and chunks of wholemeal bread. Vos realised he was starving. He'd had nothing since his lunchtime cheese and tomato sandwich. They smiled at each other across the table. There were gaps in the conversation, but not talking didn't seem to matter. The silences felt comfortable. Vos helped himself to more soup, reminding himself that he still had a main course to come.

He thought of telling Katerine about Simone Josse, the woman on the beach, but decided against it. He wasn't sure why he was being so cautious. They talked about the latest Government stalemate and speculated whether, in the end, the country might fall apart. Vos told her about his mother and the man Wouters and found himself asking Katerine's advice.

"Of course I don't know your mother," Katerine said, "but I would have thought it's up to her really, who she spends her time with. Older people are far more resilient than we think and their interest in the other sex doesn't stop just because they pass a certain age. I mean, how would you react if she asked about your love life?"

"Oh, she's always prying and I don't like it." Vos hoped he wasn't sounding petulant.

"Exactly, and I'm sure she's the same." Katerine looked almost amused.

"You're probably right," Vos said. "I've always resented her interference, even when she's been right – especially when she's been right! Perhaps I'm being a bit old fashioned about this."

"Well – you're concerned and that's good." Katerine glanced across the room for the waiter. "More beer?" she asked Vos.

They talked on through main course, the chocolate mousse and the coffee. She insisted they split the bill. As they walked along Londenstraat, she pulled up her coat collar and put her arm through his.

"Well, Mr Vos, the question is, will we see each other again? Now you have your information and your amulet is safely back in your pocket, I could be redundant." He felt confident enough to respond in similar vein.

"Ah, but I shall need a guide for what comes next. After all, this is a world I have no knowledge of, full of pitfalls and barriers. So, I'll be in need of someone to show me the way. We could meet for lunch in a few days. Is it OK if I give you a ring?"

She nodded, kissed him on the cheek, waved goodnight and disappeared down an alleyway. Vos glanced at his watch. It was past one, where had the evening gone? He rubbed his cheek where she'd kissed him. Had that really happened? Perhaps his luck was changing. Then his heart sank as he thought of Eddie's twins. Only four hours sleep. How would he survive?

Five

Vos thought his ribcage had collapsed. One of the six year olds had scored a direct hit on his chest. The other was doing his best to remove the bedclothes and expose him to the chilly early morning air. His head was sore and his mouth was dry. He reminded himself, for the hundredth time, to drink more water when he was out on the beer.

"Now you minxes, I'll give you two minutes to hide and then I'm coming after you."

The kids leapt off the bed and fled from the room. Vos collapsed back on to the pillow and savoured a few moments' rest before wearily rising, putting on his dressing gown and calling out that he was starting his hunt. He crept along the hallway and pushed open the living room door. He caught sight of a small foot, not quite hidden by the bookcase and decided to ignore it. It was too early in the game to pounce. He backed out of the room quietly and made his way to the kitchen. He poured himself a glass of water and downed it in one. The sliding cupboard in the hallway was not fully closed. He made some low growling noises and waited. A small face emerged through the gap in the door, screamed and then immediately drew back.

"Thought you might be needing this, Dad." Eddie appeared and handed him a cup of milky coffee. "What time did you get in this morning and was she nice?"

"Hey – you're as bad as your grandma! Not that late and mind your own business. How's the bar doing?"

"Not so bad. I think we might have weathered the storm, takings are on the up and I've got rid of that chef at last – you remember, you met him last time you were here. A pig of a man!"

"How could I forget? You got a new man in?"

"A new woman actually and she's really good. Mind you, Sibilla's not so pleased, but she'll come round."

"Hello Harry. Come round to what?" Sibilla's voice emerged from the bedroom.

"To the idea that the new chef's not my type," Eddie called out to his wife. "Isn't it time you were up, or have you been sacked?"

"I'm working at home this morning, once you've taken the kids to kindergarten. I can't start with them here."

Eddie began to put the breakfast things out, bread, cheese, cold meats, chocolate spread, corn flakes, orange juice and more coffee.

"Hadn't you better go and find the boys, Dad – otherwise they'll stay hidden forever?" Vos crept out of the room, made a few bear growls which were closely followed by shrieking in stereo.

"Go and get your school bags ready boys," Eddie shouted. He made omelettes for himself and his father. Sibilla sat at the kitchen table in her dressing gown, drank her coffee but didn't eat. She asked Vos what he'd been up to in Antwerp and he told her about the amulet he'd found, but not about the body. She asked him if he'd been on a date with his 'friend' from the university. He always found it easy talking to his daughter-in-law.

"I suppose it was a date really. She's very nice. That's the reason I was back here so late. I hope I didn't disturb you two. We just stayed at the restaurant talking." Sibilla looked across the table to her husband and raised her eyebrows.

"You old folk! There's really no stopping you." She ducked to avoid the piece of bread roll that Vos threw across the table.

"Have you heard from Kim at all, Dad? She seems to have been very quiet which is never a good sign."

"Now you mention it, she hasn't been in touch. But then I haven't phoned her either. I must do that." Vos never relished phone calls with his daughter. They were always 'difficult'.

"When are you going back home?" Eddie asked.

"I thought I'd stick around this morning and call in at your bar for a bit of lunch. Don't worry, Sibilla, I won't be under your feet. I've got to take the car in to the garage – problems with the clutch. I'll see you at one, Eddie, if that's OK?"

"Sure. Those boys have gone very quiet. We're going to be late for school again."

+ + +

Rodenbach relaxed for the first time in days. He'd got rid of the body and he'd spoken to Hendrickx, emphasising that Daems had just been defending himself. Hendrickx had lost his temper on the phone, but it hadn't stopped him giving out the details of the next shipment. Hendrickx was the key link in the supply chain. Rodenbach knew that without him, he'd get no business.

His job was to pick the migrants up from the coaster and shuttle them on to their ultimate destination. Sometimes this was Zeebrugge or Oostende, but more often than not it was Antwerp. This involved sailing up the Scheldt, where the merchandise was landed under cover of darkness. He knew all the tiny jetties along the coast and their tide times and he kept in radio contact with his onshore driver to arrange the details of each landing rendezvous with the minimum of notice.

Rodenbach pulled on his cigar, slowly released the bluish smoke and watched as it curled its way up to the rafters of the warehouse roof. His relaxed mood began to change as he recalled the interfering woman who'd been on the beach. Could he be sure that she'd keep her mouth shut? He decided his message needed reinforcing – a job for Daems. After all, he'd created the mess and it was up to him to make sure it was properly cleared up.

+ + +

Vos still used the same backstreet garage near Berchem Station that his father had used when he'd lived in Antwerp. The two brothers who ran the place were in their seventies, but seemed to have no thoughts of retirement. They dressed almost identically, oil-stained overalls, black beanie hats, and large boots with steel toe caps. Vos explained about the Vectra's clutch problem to the taller of the brothers who looked at his watch and asked him to come back in about an hour, by which time he'd be able to give him his diagnosis – good or bad.

Vos walked to his favourite street, nearby, which was full of art nouveau houses from the early twentieth century, each trying to outdo the next with frills and decorations. He ambled up and down until he felt he might be looking suspicious, then retired to a small café to top up his caffeine intake and phone Simone Josse. There was no answer and he left a message asking her to call. As he replaced the phone in his pocket, his fingers touched the card that Katerine had given him the previous evening, with the contact details for the man called Jalloh. Vos pulled his phone out again and dialled the number. He let it ring and eventually a gruff voice answered.

"Jalloh." Vos realised he hadn't really prepared himself for the call and didn't know how much to confide in the man.

"Mr Jalloh, you don't know me but I'm a friend of Katerine Verlinden." He hoped he wasn't stretching a point with this statement. But yes, after all, she was a friend even if he'd only met her twice – so far.

"And?" Another curt response. Perhaps the guy didn't do sentences.

"Er, well it's a bit complicated. Sorry – are you still there?" Vos thought for a moment that he was speaking to the ether. He heard a grunt at the other end of the line. He told Jalloh about the amulet and its likely origins. He didn't say anything about the body.

"What do you want me to do?" Blunt, terse, almost bored.

"I'd like to come and talk to you, show you the amulet, get your opinion."

"OK. When?"

"Tomorrow, at noon, if possible." Vos knew he'd need a lie-in in the morning, rather than another early start. "Where are you based?"

"I'll come to you. Give me your address." Vos gave him the details and asked if the man needed directions. "No. I have a satnav. That's all I need." The line went dead. Vos wondered if he wanted this man to come to his house. After all he really knew nothing about him.

The café proprietor stared at Vos, as if daring him to make another call. Perhaps he had been using the place more as a public phone box. Vos pocketed the phone and ordered a coffee. There were photographs of art nouveau houses around the café walls and Vos made a point of studying them carefully, trying to win back a little favour with the man behind the counter.

It felt almost warm when Vos stepped out of the café and made his way back to the garage. The downpour seemed to come out of nowhere and Vos ducked into a shop doorway to wait for it to pass. He tried Simone's number again while he waited. The raindrops bounced off the pavement in front of him and he stepped further back into the doorway. The shop doorbell rang and a customer emerged, took one look at the rain and retreated, cursing. Vos switched off his phone. He decided he'd drive out to

Simone's house, once he got his car back, and hope to catch her in. She'd told him she lived up in the Kempen marshes, near Geel. As it happened, his brother Pieter lived nearby and Vos thought he could take the opportunity to drop in. He didn't really like the area, found the marshes depressing. It was very popular with bird-watchers, but he'd never been that interested in birds.

+ + +

"Bad news I'm afraid, Harry. Forget about the clutch problem. To put it in technical terms, your Vectra's knackered. I mean – you've had the thing for years, haven't you? Cylinder head gasket has gone – it must have just happened. There's a crack in the engine block, and it ain't going to be worth your while repairing it." The mechanic bit into an apple and chewed slowly, not seeming to notice the streaks of oil covering the white flesh. "I can lend you a motor if you like till you get yourself sorted out – that Peugeot over there, the one that looks like a van."

Vos couldn't think straight. He had nothing saved up for a replacement vehicle. He'd never been any good at saving. Would the bank give him a loan – all he had was his pension? But he couldn't really manage without a car. He looked at the grey Peugeot.

"That'll be just the job, thanks. I'll let you know when I've got some cash together to buy another car. Will it be OK using this for a week or so?"

"Take your time, Harry. No rush. Here, let's give the insurers a ring just to straighten things up."

The driving position was higher than his Opel, better in fact. After his extended lunch at Eddie's bar, he headed out of Antwerp along the E313, through slow moving traffic towards Hasselt. There'd been an accident, nothing serious, just enough to hold everyone up.

Vos thought about how he'd pay for a new car and decided he'd have to sell a couple of paintings. They'd been a financial lifeline for him and he still had a few left. One of his father's old school friends had been a struggling artist for most of his life. Vos senior had bailed him out many a time and even provided lodgings for him, when things had been really tough. The friend had paid him back in paintings which, at the time, had been worth no more than a few francs each. When he'd inherited them on his father's death, Vos had regarded the paintings as more of a joke than anything else. But then the artist had been 'discovered' and almost overnight, his primitive paintings became sought after. Vos hadn't been able to believe his luck.

The traffic congestion gradually eased. On the spur of the moment, Vos decided to take a diversion before driving on to Geel. He stopped at a roadside stall and bought tulips and daffodils. When he reached the cemetery on the outskirts of Heist, he pulled into the car park and walked along the grassy path to Margriet's grave. He didn't visit often – not often enough he told himself. He removed the dead flowers from the two vases, filled them with water from the standpipe and arranged the new flowers as best he could. He sat on the wooden bench in the sun and told his wife that he was worried about his mother. He talked on for a few minutes, felt better for it and thanked his wife.

As he walked back to his car, his phone rang. It was a woman wanting help in tracing her daughter who'd been last heard of in Aalst. Vos was in two minds. He didn't like turning work down, but he felt that his current job was as much as he could handle, perhaps more than he could handle. He told the woman that, regrettably, because of pressures of work he wouldn't be able to take on her case. She was not pleased and he ended the call abruptly to escape her tirade.

He backtracked through the lanes to the E313, took the Geel turnoff, went through the town and headed for the marshes beyond. He drummed his fingers on the steering wheel as he waited for the lights to change at some minor road works. Simone Josse's house was just beyond the lights, set back from the road, built on a small rise. There was a car in the drive which looked hopeful. Vos lifted the brass lion's head on the front door knocker and rapped twice. He was an experienced door-knocker and felt the house sounded empty. He was right. There was no answer. He turned back along the road towards Geel and stopped at the first house he saw. An elderly woman came to the door, all suspicion and irritation. Vos asked if she knew the whereabouts of her neighbour.

"Can I ask your name please?" The woman's voice was confident. Vos decided it was an occasion for one of his business cards. The wording on the card was concise and to the point. *H. Vos – Confidential Investigator. Discretion is my watchword.* The woman stared at the card and Vos wasn't convinced she could actually read it. He thought she probably needed her glasses. The frost melted a little and Vos took his chance.

"Yes, I'm doing a little investigating for Mrs Josse."

"Actually it's Miss Josse." The neighbour spoke in an educated manner and Vos could imagine her correcting his grammar, should he slip up.

"Oh, I'm sorry. Let me explain. I'm carrying out some confidential work for Miss Josse and I wanted to update her. It's rather urgent you see. I've tried ringing her a few times, with no success, so I thought I'd try and catch her at home. Do you have any idea when she might be back?"

"I'm afraid I don't, but let me tell you what happened. It was rather peculiar." She looked around carefully and then dropped her voice as if an eavesdropper might be lurking in the trim hedgerow. "A man knocked on her door this morning. Well, actually more of a hammer than a knock. That's why I was able to hear it." Vos pictured the woman peering around her net curtains, eyes on stalks. "He was a large man and he was coloured."

"You mean black?" Vos cut in.

"Oh, yes, I suppose I do. I'm not very good at keeping up with these things. We don't see many foreign people around here, so I couldn't help noticing him. He seemed a little agitated and, I have to say, I was worried. But then Miss Josse came out of the house and climbed into his car and they drove off that way," she said, pointing towards Geel. "She's not been in that house long and I don't know much about her, but I think she may have been in Africa in the past, lived there, I mean."

"And what did this man look like?"

"Oh, I've never been much good at descriptions."

"Well, did he look like a Moroccan for example?"

"No, he didn't. He was blacker than that and tall and he had bushy hair."

"An afro?"

"Yes, that's it, an afro."

"Thank you. Well I'm sorry to have disturbed you." Vos thought the woman still seemed pre-occupied with something. "Is there anything else you can tell me?"

"Well I did get his number plate. I'm not sure I should pass it on to you really. After all it's probably all very innocent. It's just that I felt apprehensive. It wasn't entirely clear to me that she went of her own accord." Vos wasn't sure what, if anything, he'd do with the information but he thought it might come in useful.

"So – would you be willing to give me the number?" The woman recited the details and he made a note of them. "You remembered it," he said. "You didn't have to write it down?"

"Oh yes. We used to learn all sorts of thing by rote at school you know. I can still recite Timmermans."

Vos couldn't remember a single one of the poet's works, but he was impressed by the woman. There was more to her than he'd thought.

He was just about to say his farewells when he thought about the dog, the dog that had been on the beach with Simone Josse. He tried to recall its name.

"By the way, did she have the dog with her when she left?"

"No she didn't. That didn't cross my mind. I do hope Barto's not stuck in the house on his own. He has a tremendous bark."

"I think he'd have sounded off when I rang the bell just now."

He drove away from Geel, through the flat watery lands towards the shared bungalow where his brother lived. When he arrived he was told that Pieter was out for the day. Vos drove home into the setting sun which cast a pinkish glow over the still leafless trees. It reminded Vos of a painting he'd seen in a gallery, although he couldn't bring to mind which one. A pair of wading birds took off, startled by the sound of Vos' passing car and flew low over the marshy ground.

1969

My sentence was eighteen months, but they're letting me out after twelve, for good behaviour. The first two weeks were the worst. I couldn't sleep and two of the other inmates were after me. They'd heard about the way I'd floored the lad on the dockside and were up for testing me. In the end I was caught by one of them in a corridor. He slapped the side of my face. Before I'd realised what was happening, he was down. He never touched me again and the word got around. I was up before the Superintendent and was never so scared in my life. He spoke harshly to me and threatened a transfer to an adult prison. But my only punishment was enrolment with the boxing club. Skip was my saviour. I think he saw my talents but knew I'd get nowhere unless I cooled it. That was what he worked on. He'd provoke me time and again and my job was not to respond. It was almost impossible at first but gradually I got the hang of it. Skip also ran the car maintenance classes and I signed up for them. I took to it straight away and spent hours in the workshop with another lad rebuilding a sports car. We never got to drive it, but that engine sounded really sweet.

Dad's coming for me today. We had a really difficult patch when we weren't talking, but it was another thing that Skip helped me to sort out. Dad works in the bus factory now. He decided to move the family out of Antwerp, mainly for my benefit as he didn't want me getting back into old habits or trying to settle old scores. He got a job in the bus factory near this place called Heist. He's pulled a few strings and arranged an interview for me with a firm called De Backer, one of the bus factory suppliers – told them about my workshop skills. Amazingly they're OK with my criminal record. I think that must be down to Skip's reference.

The gate opens and Dad's there, waiting. He's never been at all physical, but he gives me a big hug and tries to pretend there aren't tears in his eyes. We drive to Heist which takes about an hour. The new house is nice and it's got a big garden. In the garage there's a workbench and a full set of tools.

I ask Dad where my brother Pieter is. He looks away, almost ashamed and tells me that things got very difficult. They'd not been able to cope and he's had to go to the big hospital. I'm devastated and wonder if it would have been different if I'd been at home. I'd usually been able to get through to him, calm him down when he'd started to get out of hand. Dad reads my thoughts and tells me it was nothing to do with me being away. The doctor says that it's not unusual for people with Pieter's condition.

A couple of days later we go to the hospital to visit. It's very large and very forbidding, three storeys high with strange looking towers and turrets. There are doors and locks and big bundles of keys everywhere. When we finally get through to Pieter's wing, he looks puzzled, wants to know why I haven't been to see him. Of course Dad has explained to him about me being away. He shows me his bed in a large ward, like a dormitory. He's got a few things of his own on the bedside cabinet but mostly the place is very impersonal. Wherever we walk we can hear people shouting, sometimes screaming. It's much more difficult for me than it was being in the youth prison. I can't wait to leave. As we're going, Pieter grabs my arm and asks me to take him home. It breaks my heart.

Six

Ryck had done a good job of breaking up the soil to form a fine tilth. Vos placed the tubers neatly in line, completed the row and heaped the soil into a ridge. He'd always loved potatoes, one of the reasons he was overweight, his sister had once helpfully informed him. He decided he'd plant the onions next and then beetroot, carrots and broad beans. He stopped work and stretched his back. His leg was aching, but only in a normal way. He needed a coffee.

As the kettle was boiling, he heard the sound of the key in the door.

"Want a coffee, Ryck?" Vos shouted.

"Is the Pope a catholic?"

Vos poured out two cups and set them on the table.

"So, what's new then?" he asked.

"I've got the address of that feller who's seeing Grandma," Ryck said. "Someone in *Het Waterhuis* told me last night."

"What's the man called again?"

"Wouters. The man in the bar said he's OK. I think you're worrying for nothing."

"I like worrying. Maybe I'll pay him a visit."

"Don't do anything silly, Uncle."

Vos couldn't tell whether his nephew was being serious. He let the comment go.

"I see you've got some of the spuds in." Ryck said. "What's next?"

"I've just been thinking about that. Do you fancy doing some onions?"

"Yes, but it won't be for a couple of days. I've got some more work on. A woman out at Lier wants her living room completely re-done. Should be a nice little earner and I need the money." Ryck picked up a tea towel and dried the mugs and plates that were sitting on the draining board. "How about the weekend – will that be soon enough?"

Vos nodded and poured out the coffee. Ryck went for the biscuits and Vos resisted, knowing he'd need to up his dieting game if he was ever to get anywhere.

The doorbell rang. Vos was puzzled. Was he expecting anyone? Ryck went to open the door.

"Are you Vos? I expected someone older."

"No, it's my uncle you'll want. I'll get him."

Vos had moved into the hallway and peered over his nephew's shoulder. He saw the man, heard the voice and the phone call came back to him. Of course, they had an appointment. Was it really noon already?

"Come in, Mr Jalloh, come in." Jalloh wiped his large, expensive-looking shoes on the doormat and followed Vos into the kitchen. Vos wondered fleetingly whether this was a front room occasion but then thought better of it. Most things happened in the kitchen in the Vos household. "Coffee?" Jalloh nodded and Vos fetched a third mug.

"I'll be going then. See you on Saturday," Ryck said as he waved vaguely in the direction of his uncle and went out of the back door.

"I can see the family resemblance." Jalloh said.

Vos was surprised. It was the first time he'd heard the man speak more than two words together.

"I'll just get the amulet." Vos left the kitchen and then couldn't remember where he'd put the bracelet. Somewhere safe was all he could remember.

"I just need to go to the toilet," he shouted through to the kitchen. "Help yourself to biscuits." He sat thinking. Desk, no, cupboard, no, under the bed, no, loft, certainly not – he found it more and more difficult to get up there. Then he realised that he'd never taken the amulet out of his jacket pocket. He pulled the flush, washed his hands from habit and returned to the kitchen.

"So, Mr Jalloh, what should I call you? What's your first name?"

"Just call me J. Can we talk in French?" It was more of a statement than a question. "My Flemish is not good. I've only been in the country twenty years." Vos thought he discerned the faint outline of a smile on Jalloh's face. Perhaps he did do humour.

"That's fine. My French is OK. I learnt it from my grandmother, so it tends to be a little old-fashioned. She was from Charleroi – my grandfather was a miner there." Vos wasn't quite sure why he'd mentioned this random piece of information, but Jalloh seemed to brighten.

"My father also – a miner I mean. In the copper mines when we were still colonised. Was your grandfather a coal miner?"

"He was. He died in a pit accident when I was about ten."

"I'm sorry to hear that. I had two uncles who also died in accidents. It's very hard on the families and no money coming in as well."

Vos topped up the coffee mugs and placed the amulet on the table. Jalloh picked it up and examined it carefully. He pulled a small magnifying glass out of his jacket pocket and looked at the amulet again. He spoke in a language Vos had never heard before – a single sentence.

"May the spirit go with you," he said, looking at Vos. "That's the traditional response to the inscription on the amulet which is written in Kingwana. It says *Protect me for I must travel afar*. There are two other words which are not in Kingwana. I'm not sure which of the tribal dialects they've used. Once I find that out we'll know more or less where this amulet came from. Here, I have a map. I can show you roughly where we are talking about. It will be somewhere not far from Lubumbashi."

Jalloh reached into his leather satchel and pulled out a large map of the Democratic Republic of Congo. He cleared away plates and mugs and opened the map out onto the table. He pointed out the Katanga Province. "Of course this is a huge area, but once I can identify the local dialect and the type of malachite used, we can narrow things down. Katerine – a very nice woman – she told me you found the amulet on a beach. Is that right?"

Vos nodded. "Near De Haan. It was half buried in the sand." Vos was still undecided as to whether to go any further. He didn't know Jalloh and only had Katerine's recommendation that he would be worth talking to. But he knew from his previous cases that he wouldn't get anywhere without taking a few risks. He'd learnt to follow his hunches. "There's a bit more to this story. Would you like a drink while we talk – a beer or a jenever?"

"A jenever would be good. Do you have blackcurrant?"

Vos fetched the bottle and poured two small glasses. Jalloh downed his in one and Vos topped it up. He told the story of the body on the beach and its disappearance. Jalloh sat thinking, savouring his second glass of gin.

"People-smuggling, I would guess," he said finally. "It's a great shame to get so near and then fail. It's very difficult to get here legally, there are so few permits. Some of them try the overland route across Europe, which is safer but less successful. Others come by sea, for Belgium usually through Antwerp. There are more who go to France. It's not easy there for Congolese, but it's better than here in Belgium. It's the old colonial legacy. The country doesn't want a reminder of its past. It is a good thing that you are trying to find out how one of my brothers met his death. You need to talk to my friend. He knows all about people-smuggling. Can you come with me now? We can drive to Brussels."

Vos' caution seemed to be evaporating. He sensed this was the way forward. He phoned Ryck and left a message about his unexpected trip and told him he hoped to be back for a doctor's appointment he had in the morning. They left in Jalloh's Audi, Vos sinking back into the soft leather seat, the volume of the Afro-beat CD ruling out any possibility of conversation.

+ + +

The mobile was ringing.

"Ignore it, Leo. Let it go to voicemail." Sabina tried to wrap herself more tightly around Rodenbach, but he moved to disentangle himself. "If you answer it, I won't be available by the time you've finished!" He hesitated briefly and felt the softness of the skin on her thigh. But he knew it would be Daems phoning and he might have news about the beach woman. Sabina aimed a kick at her partner as he struggled out of bed. She got up, slipped on a thin dressing gown and a pair of pink fluffy slippers and disappeared into the galley kitchen, where she moved pans about, as noisily as possible.

"What have you got?" Rodenbach said sharply.

"Something and nothing really," Daems said, knowing he was at risk of pissing off his boss. He continued hurriedly. "I've got a man keeping an eye on things for me."

"What do you mean? Get to the fucking point, will you?"

"OK, calm down. He's doing a repair job on the road just next to the woman's house. I slipped him a fifty and he's my watchman."

Rodenbach had to admit that this was a good move by Daems, who was not particularly known for his wits.

"There've been two interesting visitors. The first one was a large black man in an Opel who left a few minutes later with the woman in the passenger seat. The second one was limping and looked like a pensioner, maybe a friend of hers. Obviously she wasn't in by then, so he goes next door to some other old biddy. They have a chat for a while and then he leaves. My roadman phoned and gave me descriptions and number plates. I used your contact, like you told me, to get details of the owners from the plates and here's the odd thing. The black guy's car is apparently owned by some lecturer geezer at one of the unis in Brussels. Except this feller's out of the country on some sort of lecture tour. They wouldn't tell me where. So either someone's nicked the motor or borrowed it."

"And what about the other car?"

"Well, that's just it – another dead end. Turns out it's owned by this garage in Antwerp. I phoned up the owner and he blanks me. Tells me to bugger off basically. I'm thinking I should pay him a visit. He sounded ancient so he should be a pushover. What do you think?"

Rodenbach groaned. Why was everything always so complicated? Was it worth pursuing? After all he had put the fear of God into the woman. Maybe that was enough. On the other hand, she was the weak link.

"Yes, go ahead and put the squeeze on the garage owner, only don't go too far. We don't want another body on our hands." Rodenbach felt weary and shuffled back to bed. He'd felt under the weather for a while. He tried to ignore the continuing sounds of mayhem coming from the kitchen.

+ + +

Daems didn't like Rodenbach, but he liked his money. His chances of getting a job anywhere else were slim – no skills, no qualifications, and a prison record. He liked Sabina though and tried to spend as much time as possible around her, even though he knew it annoyed her.

He rode through the Antwerp streets until he reached Berchem station. It took him three attempts to find the right back street. He spotted the feeble neon sign above the double doors of the garage and pulled the bike up on to the pavement. An old man was closing up for the night. Just in time, Daems thought. He caught the man by the arm, pushed him inside the door and told him to co-operate. When he demanded to know who'd been driving the Peugeot, the garage owner looked at him as if he were mad.

"So you're the idiot who was on the phone this afternoon. What's so special about that bloody Peugeot? One of my customers has borrowed it while his car's being repaired and I'm not telling you who it is, however much you threaten me."

"You OK, Boss?" Daems heard the shout from the back of the garage and then, in the dim light, saw the outline of a large man in overalls, carrying what looked like a monkey wrench. Daems made a quick decision. He didn't think he could take this man on, especially as the old geezer would no doubt be snapping at his heels. He ran from the garage, jumped on his bike and sped off. He liked a fight, but only when the odds were heavily stacked in his favour. Still at least he'd found out that the Peugeot had been borrowed by a customer. He decided to return to the garage after dark and have a snoop through their records, without risk of disturbance. His tools were in the bike pannier and the lock on the garage doors had looked pretty basic. He drove on slowly through the dark streets, looking for a quiet bar to while away an hour or two.

+ + +

Vos looked out of the car window. It was an area of Brussels he didn't really know. He asked Jalloh where they were.

"Matonge is what we call it, Porte de Namur you probably know." Vos nodded. "We have also a Matonge back home in Kinshasa. This is where we Congolese hang out."

Vos watched as Jalloh punched a number into his phone, balanced the mobile in the crook of his neck and spoke rapidly in French. Vos caught the gist of the conversation, the confirmation of their rendezvous. Jalloh braked hard and pulled up in front of a derelict site, removed two traffic cones from the edge of the plot and drove onto the rough ground. He replaced the cones and beckoned to Vos to follow him into the adjacent cafe. The cafe was almost full and it was difficult to make themselves heard. Jalloh bought drinks and they joined a man sitting on his own at a small table next to the toilets. There was much back-slapping before they settled down. Jalloh did the introductions in French. The man's name was Kip, which Vos assumed was a nickname.

"So you want to trace one of the brothers, I understand." Kip's French was heavily accented and difficult to follow. Vos had to guess the meaning of some of his comments. "I should tell you that it is dangerous territory you are entering. You need to be careful. There's a lot of money involved in smuggling and the operators won't take kindly to someone poking their nose in where it's not wanted." He paused to sip his drink. "Because of where you found the body, I'd say the two most likely suspects are an outfit run by the Durand brothers and another which goes under the name of LTrading. The Durands are based here in Brussels. They leave a very light footprint and are very hard to track down. LTrading are an oddity. Most of what they do is above board, but the word is that they're also small-time people-smugglers. They've got some kind of base in Zeebrugge, so you could start looking there. Apparently they operate under two or three other names as well, which are always changing. They're good at keeping at least one step ahead of the authorities. Do you have a shooter?" Vos had to ask Kip to repeat the question. "You know – a gun?" Vos thought that's what the man had said.

"No, no, nothing like that. I'm just an amateur. This isn't my usual sort of case."

"Good, that probably helps. You'll be naturally cautious. We may be able to help you. We don't like these guys, but at the same time we don't want our brothers caught. So it's a difficult game for us to play. You want to hear some music now?"

Vos was surprised at the sudden change in the conversation. There were still questions he wanted to ask Kip, but maybe there'd be a chance for that later. He told his two hosts that music would be good and they led the way out of the café and along a well-lit main street, stopping frequently to greet acquaintances.

Kip bought three trays of beef and greens in a peanut sauce at a stall with a flimsy plastic roof which flapped in the breeze. They used plastic forks to scoop up the hot spicy food off thin paper plates. Vos found it was something of a balancing act to keep the food on the plate at the same time as trying to pick his way through the stalls, hawkers, buskers and stray dogs and keep up with Kip and Jalloh.

They turned off the bustling street into a dark, narrow alley. The paving slabs were uneven and there were puddles everywhere. Vos lost the last of his spicy beef as it slid off the plate and disappeared into one of the deeper pools. As they turned yet another corner in the alleyway, he heard the sound of music thundering out from a three storey stone building that had seen better days. A gaudy display announced the Club Highlife. The burly guys on the door nodded to Kip and the three of them stepped through the narrow doorway.

The place was dimly lit by the occasional wall-light. Jalloh headed over towards the bar. Conversation was almost impossible. Vos exchanged the odd word with Kip and watched the punters on the tiny dance floor. He thought he recognised one of the numbers the band was playing and asked Kip what it was. At the third attempt he managed to pick up that the band was a Manu Dibango tribute group. As the sax blared out, the dancers performed minor miracles in such a small space. There was a huge cheer as the band swept into a new number, obviously a local favourite. Jalloh emerged through the crowd carrying three overfull glasses and grasping two packets of nuts between his teeth. They found a small space next to the fire exit and clinked glasses.

"I've just been speaking to your girlfriend," Jalloh said, his face its usual blank canvas. Vos stared uncomprehendingly at him. He was about to say he didn't have a girlfriend. He didn't expect to see Monica again. He asked Jalloh what he meant. "The lovely Katerine. She's just been on the phone." Vos was now intrigued.

"What did she say?"

"That she likes you. It sounds promising I must say."

"Why was she on the phone?"

"Oh, she just wanted to know how our discussion had gone, so I told her."

Kip was captured by a tall, slender woman and removed to the dance area. The two of them seemed to melt together. It was a slower number which required the minimum of movement and more couples squeezed into the impossibly small space. Jalloh fetched more drinks and Vos began to sink into a state of pleasant abandon. A couple vacated their table in front of him and he slid into one of the seats, grateful to take the weight off his feet. He put his jacket on the back of the other seat to save it for Jalloh and closed his eyes, feet tapping and head nodding to the rhythm of another faster number. As he felt cool hands on his brow, he imagined he must have drifted off into a very pleasant dream and then realised that someone was standing behind his seat. He turned and saw Katerine. Where on earth had she sprung from? He'd been thinking about her as the music swirled around him and then, as if by magic, there she was.

"Hi Harry – J told me you were here having a good time so I thought I'd come and join you."

"But how did you get here – I mean so quickly?" Vos felt the question sounded a little foolish.

"By the wonders of modern transport – train and taxi! But I already knew you'd be here – Jalloh told me he'd be bringing you when I spoke to him this afternoon, so I've had plenty of time to get ready."

Vos looked at her again. She was wearing a long peasant skirt and a white blouse. He thought that she must actually fancy him if she'd travelled this far to meet up. She asked him if he wanted to dance and he told her he was a terrible dancer. She pulled him out of his seat, ignoring his protestations. They weaved their way across the crowded room to the dance area, where he was able to demonstrate, rapidly, that his comments about his dancing skills were not based on false modesty. The dancing was interspersed with more drinks.

Jalloh suggested they go back to his apartment which he said was only a short walk away. He'd collect the car in the morning. Vos walked arm in arm with Katerine. Kip was nowhere to be seen. The apartment was furnished minimally in very good taste. Jalloh showed his guest couple the spare bedroom and the bathroom and retired to his own room. Vos tumbled onto the bed and, almost immediately, fell asleep.

1977

My head is pounding and I'm getting those jagged shafts of light across my eyeballs, a sure sign of a good night that turned into a bad night. I lost track of the drink we downed and I can't remember how we got back to the hut, or how I managed to get up this morning.

I look up and see the iron ladder fixed to the rock face. Part of me says go back to the hut, but the stronger part goads me forward. Come on Harry – you can do it, I tell myself. We've done parts of the via ferrata before so I know what it's like. It's cold and I blow on my hands to try and get some circulation going.

Marc calls out to me and tells me to get moving. If it wasn't for Marc I wouldn't be here. He arranges it all, the train, the local buses, the huts. I just turn up and pay him my share. Not that he minds. He wouldn't let me anywhere near the organising side of things. I think he knows he's not the easiest man to get on with, especially at close quarters. He puts up with me because I put up with him. We've climbed together for years. It's quite a laugh really – me from the Low Countries being so keen on mountaineering. Occasionally, somebody else joins us but it never really works out. Me and Marc bicker like an old married couple. We're so used to it that we don't think it's anything out of the ordinary. We never listen to ourselves, but for anyone else it must be a pain.

The metal ladder is covered in a thin layer of frost. I say to Marc that maybe we should wait until the sun warms up a little. But as usual he's got his plan and if we delay now, it will throw out the whole day's itinerary. Typical Marc! I go along with it. We start to climb. My gloves are worn and my hands are still cold.

We complete the first climb and rest on a ledge, pouring coffee from a flask which cools almost as soon as it's in the cup. The sun makes more of an effort and a little warmth percolates through. We continue upwards. The next section is in the shade. I stare

*out across the valley which is still covered in mist. A bird hovers
below. I can't quite make it out, but it's probably a buzzard. I can
see the feathered wing tips. Marc shouts again for me to get a
move on. My head's clearing but only at about the same rate as
the mist. I'm part way up the ladder when my right hand and
my right foot slip at exactly the same moment. Normally I'd be
able to grip with my left and hang on but the slipperiness of the
ladder prevents me. I imagine what's going to happen just before it
actually does. I slither at first and then drop. I'm not sure how far
– maybe five metres onto solid rock, just where we had the coffee.
I'm thinking about the landing before it happens. At least I'm the
right way up, but that means that my legs take all the weight and
most of it on my right knee. Somehow I have a gash on the right
side of my head.*

*The fall is other-worldly and I can hear this Pink Floyd track
echoing around my head, all dreamy guitars and soft harmonies.
And then it's as if I enter another world, not the one I was climbing
in, but a world of sharp edges, unforgiving, grey, isolated. I don't feel
any pain at first, just huge relief that I'm still alive. It must be the
initial adrenaline rush. I wonder how my knee can be at such an
impossible angle.*

*Suddenly Marc is in front of me and he's brilliant. No panic, no
hesitation, no attempts at inappropriate jokes. He's talking calmly
and firmly to me. I must wait here and mustn't try to move. He
takes off his puffa jacket and wraps it around me, ignoring my
feeble protestations. He tells me he's going down the mountainside
to get help, that maybe there'll still be somebody at the hut and if
not, he'll run on to the village. When he's gone, I sink into despair as
the pain kicks in. It's excruciating. I convince myself that I'll never
be able to walk again. My thoughts churn over and over. I realise
I can't really move, even if I wanted to. I can't escape the word …
paralysis. What if…what if…*

I see myself in a wheelchair, having to live back at home. I construct a whole depressing world within seconds and then things start to fade. I can feel the sun, finally, pushing away the cold air that surrounds me, calming my shivering body. I need to stay awake and not give in to the temptation to sleep. I start to sing, anything that comes to mind, hymns I learnt at school, folk songs from the club, Beatles songs from the radio. I try to drag the words out from dark recesses but where I fail, I make them up, my rhyming nonsense spilling out over the Dolomite valley.

Marc is suddenly there again. I think I'm imagining it. The men behind him are carrying a stretcher. They put me on it, wrap me in blankets, fasten and tighten the straps. I don't know how they get me down the ladder, my eyes are firmly closed. I keep singing and the bearers join in where they know the songs. There's a flashing light on a white van and I'm pushed inside. Marc sits on the floor beside me. The journey seems endless. My singing dries up but Marc talks non-stop about anything that comes into his mind, cycling, women, boxing, beer. Then I'm in the hospital and the doctor examines me, prods and pokes me and watches my reactions. She tells me it looks like I'll need a new right knee and maybe more. She knows the question I'm going to ask before I ask it and she reassures me, you'll be OK, you'll walk again. But there's a sting in the tail – isn't there always?! They may not be able to put it all back together again exactly how it was. I may be left with a limp – permanently. I finally give in and fall asleep.

Seven

Ryck was more than halfway through his onion planting – two rows down and one to go. It was starting to rain and he needed a break. He sat in the shed, with the door open and drank from a water bottle. He broke off two pieces of chocolate from the bar in his pocket and put them both in his mouth, sucking on them until they were soft enough to chew.

He wondered if his uncle was OK. He was used to his comings and goings but he usually rang to say he'd be delayed. He checked his phone again. Nothing. The cane chair had seen better days. The hut smelt pleasantly of wood and compost. There was a row of boots in one corner, wellingtons, hiking boots, work boots. There were several waterproofs hanging on hooks to the side of the hut's only window, one or two of them looking decades old. A battered kettle stood beside a green mug with a picture of a wading bird on it. He turned the paint-spattered radio on. It was tuned to the classical music channel. He flicked the dial and found Sporza. The host was talking about some football transfer saga that had been running for weeks. Would he or wouldn't he sign at the end of the season? Ryck turned the radio off and heard a voice calling. He recognised his grandma's voice and went outside. She was standing looking at his handiwork.

"You're doing a good job here, Ryck love. You're much neater than Harry. Where is he by the way?" Ryck wasn't sure how much to say. He hadn't taken to Jalloh and had been a little concerned when he'd read his uncle's note which informed him that they'd gone off together. But he didn't want to worry his grandma unnecessarily.

"He's away visiting a friend in Brussels – he didn't say who. He said he'd be back today."

"He's always off gallivanting somewhere. Never tells me anything. I came to tell him something actually. Can you mention when he deigns to show up that I'm going to Aarschot?" Ryck was dying to ask his grandma about her alleged fancy man, Mr Wouters of Aarschot, but he didn't dare.

"I'll tell him, don't worry. Will you be back today?"

She shook her head. "No, not till tomorrow, otherwise I wouldn't have mentioned it. I'll have my mobile telephone with me if he needs to contact me. 'Bye." She walked slowly towards the garden gate and waved to Ryck before turning to watch for traffic and crossing the road. He wondered about his grandma. Could she really be staying overnight at Wouter's place? A few minutes later his phone rang and he was relieved to hear his uncle's voice.

"Hi Ryck. Yes I'm fine. Look, could you do me a big favour? I've had a call from the garage to say my car's fixed. Bit of a surprise really. I thought it was ready for the scrapyard. Apparently they found this cheap second hand engine. Anyway could you return the Peugeot and pick up my car? I'm a little tied up at present and won't be back until tomorrow. You're covered on their insurance and I'll settle up with the garage, so you don't need to worry about paying them. Would you be able to do that? Oh and how's the garden going?"

Ryck told his uncle that he'd sort the car out and that the onions were going in nicely. It was only when the call was over that he realised he hadn't told him about his grandma's little jaunt to Aarschot. He considered calling him back but then decided against it. Why worry him unnecessarily if he wasn't going to be around until tomorrow anyway?

It was a while since he'd been to Antwerp and he'd enjoy the drive.

+ + +

Vos placed his phone on the bedside cabinet and lay back. He put his arm around Katerine and pulled her towards him. He'd gone out like a light early that morning and had awoken embarrassed at six, dry-mouthed, with Katerine lying next to him. He couldn't remember whether anything had actually happened and sheepishly broached the subject. She wouldn't commit herself and teased him mercilessly.

"You're obviously getting past it, old man. A few drinks and even the sight of a pretty woman isn't enough to keep you awake."

"Well then, I must rectify that. We can't have that sort of tale going round sullying the reputation and good name of Harry Vos."

It was now past noon and they still hadn't left the bed except for coffee and toast and the call of nature. Jalloh had departed for work hours previously, leaving a note which told them to carry on enjoying themselves and not worry too much about the workers.

Vos couldn't believe his good fortune. He really had no idea what Katerine saw in him. He guessed that there were only a few years between them, but she was an attractive, well paid university lecturer and he was a lame, retired, factory worker. OK – he was maybe exaggerating a little, but he was still surprised and told her so. He was always self-conscious about his limp when he met somebody new. He found that people often had funny attitudes about disability, and had a tendency to treat him as a poor man who needed help and assumed that there were all sorts of things that he couldn't manage.

"So you can cope with the limp, can you?" he asked. Katerine said she didn't really understand the question.

"Of course I know it's there but it doesn't seem at all important to me. It's just another part of you. And it's not as if you're limp all over." She burst out laughing and Vos couldn't help but join in.

+ + +

Ryck pulled up by the doors of the garage in Berchem. The two elderly brothers who ran the place were standing by the side of a burnt out car, chatting and smoking.

"Not looking for a new motor are you, son?" the taller man said, grinning at his brother.

"Oh, I couldn't afford that. Too high a spec for me!" Ryck handed the Peugeot keys over to the joker and explained why it was him returning the vehicle – rather than his uncle.

"Well, I'm not surprised to hear that Harry's living it up in Brussels," the old man said. "His car's ready. It should do him for a while – we were just lucky with that engine. Tell him the Vectra's not going to last forever – but at least now it'll be the bodywork that gives up the ghost first, not the engine. We can keep a look out for a replacement. We know the sort of motor he likes." He fetched the keys for Vos' car and handed them to Ryck.

"There's something I should mention," the mechanic said. "There was a man snooping around here yesterday asking questions about who'd been driving the Peugeot you've just returned. Fancied himself as a bit of a hardman. Just keep your eyes open. He was riding a big BMW."

Ryck thanked the old man and drove off in the Vectra. He thought about spending some time in Antwerp, but decided to head for Harry's place – and the onion bed. He wondered why anyone would be interested in the Peugeot – or Harry.

He took it steady driving out of Antwerp. He'd gone about fifteen kilometres when he glanced in his rear view mirror and spotted a large BMW motor bike, two or three vehicles behind him. His imagination went into overdrive. He looked again. It was a K1200. Ryck had a thing about bikes. He'd always wanted a big powerful machine, but had never had enough money. Was this the hardcase that the mechanic had told him about or was it just a coincidence?

He felt slightly disappointed when the BMW failed to follow him as he turned onto the back road leading to his uncle's house. The mystery of the BMW rider had been intriguing him.

Ryck pulled on to the hardstanding next to the garden shed. He unlocked the front door of the house, took his shoes off, turned the heating on and filled the kettle. He'd missed an afternoon's decoration work on the other side of Heist and realised he'd have to start early the next morning if he was to catch up. As he was making himself an instant coffee he heard a knock on the front door. When Ryck opened up, he knew straight away that the man with the bulging neck muscles and the bike helmet was his all too real mystery rider.

"Police!" the man said, spitting out the word. "I have reason to believe you were recently the driver of a car involved in a hit and run accident – a Peugeot Partner," the man continued. "Is that correct?"

"Where's your ID?" Ryck asked. He wasn't convinced that the man really was a police officer, but he'd had a few run-ins with them in the past, mainly over drugs, and he knew they came in all shapes and sizes. The man pulled a laminated card out of the top pocket of his leather jacket which identified him as Inspector Lokeren.

"Now – answer my question!" Lokeren said. Ryck hesitated. "Let's do this inside," the detective stated firmly.

Ryck was wary of letting this man inside the house. But if he continued to stand on the doorstep he'd inevitably arouse the interest of the nosy woman who lived next door. Reluctantly he ushered Lokeren into the kitchen wondering how to handle things. They sat at opposite sides of the table.

"So why did you visit the old woman just outside Geel yesterday?" The question came out of the blue and Ryck wondered what it had to do with the alleged hit and run.

"I didn't drive the car yesterday. It must have been my uncle." The words spilled out before he realised he'd dropped his uncle into it. He should have kept his mouth shut.

"And where's your uncle now?" Lokeren asked. Ryck explained that he was away on business.

"Let me just check my phone. It's been off. He may have texted about when he'll be back." Ryck fiddled with the phone and held it up as if checking for texts. "No, there's nothing from him. I'll text him now to find out when he'll be back. What did you say the woman near Geel was called?"

"I didn't, but her name's Josse."

Ryck drafted a text to a number he made up.

"Let me see that," Lokeren called out. He seemed satisfied with what had been written and demanded a pen to write down the number. Ryck wondered again what was keeping his uncle in Brussels.

"Why don't you give me your number?" he asked Lokeren. "Then I can phone you when my uncle gets back."

"That won't be necessary. I have his number, don't I?"

Lokeren rose from his seat and headed for the front door. He disappeared out into the rain and a few moments later Ryck heard a powerful bike engine burst into life. He picked up his phone and sent a text to his uncle's number.

+ + +

Katerine had just left Jalloh's flat and had taken a taxi to the station. Vos was sprawled on the big leather sofa, savouring his good fortune. He picked up Jalloh's newspaper and flicked through it. He started with the sports news on the back pages, checked the results of the mid-week matches and read an article speculating on the country's World Cup prospects. As he turned to the front page, the face of Simone Josse stared out at him and then his eye caught the headline. 'Lawyer Found Dead.' Vos' feelings of contentment and goodwill vanished instantly. Hands shaking, he read on.

"Ms Simone Josse, a lawyer and specialist in West African affairs, was found dead yesterday in a Brussels apartment. She lived and worked for many years in the DRC and had strong connections with migrant organisations in Brussels. A police spokeswoman said that the circumstances of her death were suspicious, but made no further comment."

The article went on to quote two Congolese migrants, both praising the dedication and energy of her work on legal rights.

Vos was stunned. He fetched a glass of water from the kitchen and reread the article. He recalled her comment about the man who'd removed the dead body from the beach near De Haan. The man had really frightened her. Had he tracked her down and killed her, just like that, in cold blood?

Vos felt vulnerable. If they could track her down, would they also find him? His links with Simone Josse had been very limited, but he'd made that abortive visit to her house and she'd been to his own house.

He needed to get home urgently. He followed the instructions that Jalloh had left him for locking up and setting the alarm and made his way to the station.

1988

Dad and I are heading for the Ardennes. I've finally persuaded him that walking will be good for him. We've got a small house booked near La Roche. I've bought him a proper waterproof and some decent boots. I'm OK as long as I use a couple of sticks. They call them trekking poles these days.

I can't thank Dad enough for sorting me out all those years ago. It's hard to believe that I've been at De Backers now for nearly twenty years and have become a bit of a specialist. The money's good, which really helps with two kids to bring up. We've managed to buy a bungalow only ten minutes walk from mum and dad's place.

I've had to give up the boxing and nowadays, my cycling is limited to trips to the newsagents and back. I haven't had the road bike out for years. But the walking has really taken over.

"Where do we turn off, Harry?" Dad is peering ahead trying to keep the sun out of his eyes. I check the map and tell him we need the next junction – the N89. He's a careful driver and doesn't get annoyed by the antics of others. We leave the A26 and head west. The traffic thins out. I glance at the note that gives directions to the holiday house. As usual, I've scribbled it down in too much of a hurry. It takes me a while to decipher it. We take the turning to the left on to a minor road with woods on either side.

It all happens so quickly. One minute we're cruising along at 80 and the next we're bouncing down a wooded hillside. I don't even see the other car until it rams into the side of us. We seem to fall down the hillside for ever until the gap between the trees becomes too narrow and the car slams to a sickening halt. The seat belt cuts into my chest. I can hardly breathe. I look to my left. Dad is slumped in his seat. The engine is racing, his foot stuck on the accelerator. The roof on his side has buckled from the force of hitting the tree.

I know instinctively that he's gone. I manage to turn off the engine and kick open the passenger door, but I don't know what to do next. I stand in the forest and look up to the canopy above. Out there it is utterly quiet. Inside my head the engine is still roaring. I don't try to hold back the tears.

It's hard work walking back up the steep slope to the road. I move mechanically until I reach the top and stand dazed for minutes. I'm slowly aware that a tractor is bearing down on me and I wave my arms wildly. It's only when the vehicle shudders to a halt that I realise I'm standing in the middle of the road. The driver looks like he's about to curse me, until he sees I'm in a bad way. He says he'll drive to his house and phone the people that need to be phoned. Then he'll come and find me. I slither back down the slope to keep Dad company.

The other car didn't stop. The driver is never traced.

Eight

Daems had been on something of a high when he'd called Rodenbach to tell him about his progress. But the boss had been his usual negative self, wanting more, as always. He'd instructed Daems to go back to the house in Heist and hang around until the owner returned.

Daems wished he'd brought his car instead of the bike. The rain had started again and he felt cold and miserable. Why was this wild goose chase necessary? The body was gone, nobody would ever find it and Rodenbach had already put the frighteners on the woman. So, why couldn't he just forget about her? But the boss didn't like loose ends – and never knew when to let things go.

The house was in darkness. Daems considered breaking in, so he could take shelter, but concluded it would be too risky. There might be an alarm. He decided to wait another hour and then give up if there was still no sign of life.

+ + +

Het Waterhuis was the kind of bar Ryck hated. The bare fluorescent lights gave him a headache. The plastic-tiled floor was greasy and the polystyrene tiles on the ceiling still held traces of Christmas decorations that should have been removed months before. He sat at the bar nursing a small glass of Stella. He'd asked the

barman to give him a nod when Wouters came in. The barman
had only agreed reluctantly, as if he'd been asked to be complicit
in something illegal. He'd cheered up and lost his scruples once
Ryck had showed him a ten euro note.

Ryck ran a professional eye over the bar's décor. The paintwork
was a not so delicate shade of nicotine. The place had obviously
not been touched since the start of the smoking ban. He doubted
they'd have the money to freshen up the place but he thought it
might be worth touting for a bit of business. His glass was empty
and he wondered whether he should get a top-up. He needed
some Dutch courage. It wasn't every day that he interfered with his
grandma's love life. He sipped his second glass ever more slowly.
The two guys on the pool table seemed as incompetent as each
other. More than once, the white ball skied off the table and rolled
across the floor. There was an old man sitting in the corner reading
the local paper and a group of women in a huddle, in the opposite
corner, talking in low voices. The barman wasn't exactly rushed off
his feet. Ryck pretended to be absorbed with his phone. He heard
the barman cough in an exaggerated fashion and looked up. The
barman inclined his head in the direction of a newcomer who was
moving with a spring in his step to join the old man in the corner.

Ryck hadn't planned his way forward, but felt he couldn't
really go up and ask Wouters point blank whether his intentions
were honourable. He picked up his glass and walked across to
join the two men.

"Hi there! My name's Ryck. I was talking to the barman before
and he said you might be coming in, Mr Wouters. You see I'm Mrs
Vos' grandson and she told me about you." Ryck was conscious
that this comment could be taken the wrong way and he hoped
he hadn't got off on the wrong foot.

"Oh, I'm very pleased to meet you, Ryck. Your grandma is
a fine woman and a fine dancer. What are you drinking?" Ryck
studied Wouters' face for signs of insincerity, but saw none. He

asked for another small glass of Stella and sat down beside the old man whilst Wouters fetched the drinks.

"He's a bullshitter." Ryck was taken aback. The old man had spoken without seeming to move his lips. Ryck thought he'd have made a good ventriloquist. "He's always had the gift of the gab, but he's OK. His heart's in the right place and he's not short of a franc or two." The old man got up and shuffled off to the gents. Ryck felt that, on the whole, it had been a positive testimonial, give or take a bit of bullshitting.

Wouters was a good story teller and a congenial host. He insisted on buying the drinks and Ryck lost count of the number of times his glass was refilled. It gradually dawned on him that he was way over the limit and that he'd have to leave his Vespa in the car park behind the bar. He didn't want to pay for a taxi. When he blurted out to Wouters about his problem getting home, his host put an arm round his shoulder and told him he'd be more than welcome to stay the night at his house. Ryck felt rather awkward, but not awkward enough to refuse the offer of a bed.

He walked a little unsteadily alongside Wouters who kept up a brisk pace and seemed unaffected by the drink. They reached a small, neat, bungalow. Wouters fumbled with his keys until he found the right one and then opened the front door telling Ryck in a loud whisper to keep as quiet as possible. A light suddenly snapped on and Ryck found himself standing face to face with his grandma in her nightdress.

+ + +

It had been a slow, cold train journey with two changes and no heating. Vos walked as quickly as possible from Heist station to his house. He pushed open the garden gate and saw what looked like a tiny red light through the shed window. But after rubbing his eyes, it disappeared.

Once inside the house, he removed his shoes and searched for his slippers. He found them under the bed and went into the kitchen to make himself a sandwich. He heard the doorbell and cursed. He didn't care who it was, he didn't want to see anybody. He'd spent the whole journey worrying about Simone Josse's death and wondering if he should contact the police. The doorbell refused to stop ringing. Wearily he walked up the hallway and opened the door. The man was a complete stranger.

"Mr Vos?" The man was curt and aggressive. Vos nodded. "I'm Inspector Lokeren," the man continued. He waved an ID card in Vos' face. "I need to speak to you about a hit and run accident involving a Peugeot Partner – the same one that I know you've been driving recently."

Vos was caught off guard. He could see the curtain twitching in the window of the house next door – his snooping neighbour. He decided to let the man in to the kitchen.

"What exactly do you want to know?" Vos said, wanting to get the interview over as quickly as possible.

"Tell me why you visited the house near Geel yesterday – the old woman's house?" Vos was immediately on his guard.

"What's that got to do with a hit and run?" he asked, trying to keep calm.

"Just answer the fucking question!" Vos was taken aback by the change in Lokeren's manner. He wondered how the man knew about this.

"Look, Officer. If you must know, I called at Simone Josse's house to collect a knitting pattern. She's a friend of my mother's and they swap patterns. But she wasn't in. That's it! That's all I can tell you."

"What do you take me for?" Lokeren shouted. "You'll have to come up with a better story than that. We know she's disappeared. Give me your laptop and your phone now." His face had reddened and there was spittle at the corners of his mouth. Vos thought that the man seemed to have shed his ill-fitting detective's skin in an instant. He rose from his seat.

"Look Lokeren, I don't believe for a second that you're a cop and I'm not handing anything over to you." His voice was loud but controlled. "I want you out of my house now!"

Lokeren stood up and hit Vos hard in the stomach. Vos doubled up in pain and had to hold onto the chair to keep his footing. When he eventually straightened, Lokeren came at him again. Vos managed to parry the second blow and then caught the man with his old trademark right hook. The man crashed to the ground, catching his head on the side of the table as he fell.

There was suddenly blood everywhere. All the old demons raced back into Vos' mind. For an instant, he was a sixteen year old again, out on the cobbled road on the dockside. He knew he couldn't afford to panic. This time it had to be different. He fetched a towel and wrapped it around the man's head wound. Lokeren didn't stir. Vos placed him in the recovery position. He phoned the ambulance first and then, with great difficulty, he spoke to the police. He told them the minimum they needed to know. He tried Ryck's phone but it went straight to voicemail. He left a brief message. He couldn't think of who else to call – certainly not his mother. There was nothing more he could do, but wait for the emergency services to arrive.

He wondered if his day could get any worse.

+ + +

The cell was tiny with a small window high up. There was a single unshaded bulb, a wooden bunk with a mattress but no bedclothes and a stinking toilet in the corner. His phone and belt had been removed.

The interview had not gone well. The detective assigned to the case was young and aggressive. Vos described, as calmly

and carefully as he could, what had happened in his house. He
gradually became aware that he faced three, very large problems.

Things had begun to get very difficult when he'd mentioned
Lokeren's interest in Simone Josse. Yes he knew her, but only
slightly, yes he had visited her, but she hadn't been in and yes, as
it happened, he had been in Brussels on the night she died. But
that was just pure coincidence. The young detective looked as if
he had never heard of the concept of coincidence.

Vos' second difficulty was that there was no-one who could
provide corroboration for his version of events. He'd given the
police Katerine's phone number, but there'd been no response to
their calls and texts. He'd asked them to try Jalloh's number. They'd
left a message and made a few enquiries. They'd then proceeded
to ask Vos why he'd been staying in the house of a well-known
extremist. They asked him whether he'd met anybody else that
evening. He'd thought about mentioning Kip, but he didn't know
his real name or his phone number. And no doubt in the eyes of
the police he'd be another 'extremist'.

It was becoming obvious to Vos that the police were trying to
build up a picture of him as a suspect, not a victim.

His third problem only reinforced this image. Vos was led
again from his cell to the interview room at four in the morning.
The sergeant offered him a cup of coffee. It was quite the worst
coffee Vos had ever tasted. It stayed in the cup.

"So you have something of a record, Mr Vos." He wasn't sure
how to respond. His head ached, his stomach was worse and he
hadn't eaten since the previous lunchtime. "Quite the little thug,
weren't we – an unprovoked attack at the tender age of sixteen.
I'm glad to see you did time for it. Since then you seem to have
been quiet, or perhaps you've just been very good at covering
your aggressive tracks." Vos knew he should say something to
defend himself but he couldn't think straight and he just wanted
to sleep.

"And now this!" The detective continued relentlessly. "Your victim is still unconscious and in a bad way. We don't know whether he'll make it, so it could be a murder charge you'll be facing. What I don't understand is why you're mixed up in all this. What was your real link with Miss Josse? I'm afraid I simply don't believe your story about finding a body on a beach. We've spoken to the local police down on the coast and they just have you down as a crank. There was no body. So you better come up with something better than that if you want to save your skin."

Vos was eventually returned to his cell. He asked for some water and it arrived lukewarm, in a chipped, dirty mug. He lay on the bunk and stared at the ceiling. He tried to block out all his old fears by concentrating on the questions he needed to answer.

Who had killed Simone Josse? Who was the man who'd attacked him? Why was there no response from Katerine's phone? Where on earth was Ryck? The questions rolled round and round his head and the answers remained stubbornly elusive. Did Lokeren - or whatever he was really called - have something to do with the man who'd threatened and abducted Simone Josse at the beach? From what Lokeren had said about her 'disappearance', he didn't seem to know about her death. If he'd intended to harm her, someone had beaten him to it. That worried Vos even more.

He thought he could detect a faint lightening of the sky through the small window high above him - and hoped it wasn't wishful thinking. The pain in his stomach was intense. He pulled up his fleece and shirt to examine his stomach. For some reason there was no sign of bruising where Lokeren had hit him - at least not as yet. This was one more piece of evidence he couldn't provide. He wondered what his mother would think of it all. He hadn't even told her about the body on the shoreline, let alone all that had happened since.

His power of reason deserted him. Even worse, he couldn't put off using the foul-smelling toilet any longer.

+ + +

Ryck had just about recovered from the encounter with his grandma. Wouters had been amused and had found it difficult trying to work out which of them had looked the more shocked. Ryck had slept on the large sofa in the living room hoping and praying that he would hear no sounds from the adjacent bedroom.

He'd left the house early, as quietly as possible, and walked back to the bar to pick up his Vespa. The morning was bright and sunny and he felt there was a definite touch of spring in the air as he rode along back roads to Heist. He couldn't be sure whether he was still over the drink-drive limit and kept a wary eye open for police cars. But the roads were quiet apart from an occasional, sluggish early morning tractor. He reached his uncle's house and parked up. Because it was early he knocked rather than using his key straight away. There was no response. He went in. The kitchen was in a state. Two chairs lay on their sides and there were muddy footprints all over the floor. He righted the chairs, found a mop and bucket and gave the floor a good clean, then made coffee and toast and sat down to eat. As he ate he checked his phone. There was a late night message from his uncle. He couldn't understand how he'd missed it, but perhaps the booze had something to do with it. He played the message.

"Ryck, it's Harry." The voice sounded hoarse, uncertain and very worried. "Look, it's hard to explain everything but there's been an incident and I'm being taken in for questioning by the police. I think they're taking me to Mechelen. Can you ring the police as soon as you pick this up, find out where I am and get there as quick as you can? I need your help badly. Er…that's it. They're taking my phone off me."

Ryck choked on his toast. He downed the coffee and hunted for the spare set of keys for Vos' car, eventually finding them hidden inside a plant pot. He phoned Mechelen police station. After a long wait, he was finally put through to someone who was willing to talk to him and who confirmed that his uncle was indeed being detained there.

The roads were clogged with commuter traffic. Ryck wondered what had happened to his uncle. He assumed it was something to do with the so-called Inspector Lokeren. Had he returned and caused problems? He thought something serious must have happened if the Feds were involved, rather than the local cops in Heist. Would he be able to help? At least he could tell them something about Lokeren. He concentrated on the slow-moving traffic. He'd been to the Mechelen police station once before – a previous brush with the law – and knew there was a multi-storey car park close-by. The only spaces still available were on the very top level. He avoided the lift, ran down the concrete stairway and sprinted the two blocks to the station.

At the reception desk they were less than helpful. Only after he'd shown his driving licence, to prove his identity, would they listen to what he had to say.

They told him to sit and wait. The station was irritatingly busy. A family with two small children came in, the two parents screaming at each other about a TV. He claimed he'd bought it from a man in a bar. She told him he was a fool if he expected her to believe him ever again. Ryck felt sorry for the children who looked blankly at the floor. Two teenagers sat in corner seats and relieved their boredom by pointing and laughing at everyone who came through the door.

Eventually a uniformed officer called out Ryck's name and signalled for him to follow. He hoped his breath didn't still smell of alcohol and wished he'd taken the time to clean his teeth before he'd set off. He was led downstairs and along a series of anonymous corridors, which left him completely disorientated. The officer knocked on a door numbered 847. Ryck had an image of a whole labyrinth of offices, stretching underground.

Inside the room it was hot and stuffy and the lights were over-bright. His uncle was sitting on a grey, plastic stacking chair looking considerably worse than Ryck felt.

"OK kid, what've you got for us?" Ryck really resented this. He was twenty-nine for Christ's sake and the detective asking the question looked like he'd not long left school, but he kept his cool. It was not a time for resentment.

"Well if someone could tell me what's happened, I can tell you if I've got anything that'll help."

"You haven't been briefed?! Typical, those wasters on Intake need a kick up the backside." The detective gave a brief summary of the events of the previous evening adding that Vos was in very serious trouble, particularly as the assault victim had still not regained consciousness. Ryck approached it all calmly and logically.

"So, you basically want to know whether there's anything that backs up my uncle's version of events?" The sergeant nodded. "OK, as it happens, there is." Ryck reached in his pocket for his phone.

"Well, are you going to enlighten us, son, or are you making a phone call?" Ryck held one hand up and continued to fiddle with the phone with the other.

"Is this the man who's the so-called victim?" He held up his phone and they all peered at the photograph.

"How did you get this?" the sergeant asked aggressively. "How do you know this man?"

"Is he the victim?" Ryck repeated patiently. He noticed how his uncle's demeanour had changed completely as soon as he'd seen the photo.

"Yes of course," the detective snapped. "How did you get it?"

Ryck took his time explaining about the evening visitor at his uncle's house, how he thought the man's claim to be a police officer was bogus and how he'd managed to take a photo of Lokeren without him realising. As he took in the implications of Ryck's story, the detective looked as annoyed as if someone had scored against his favourite team in extra time.

"I texted my uncle yesterday evening, to tell him that this man Lokeren had been snooping around asking questions. Did you get the text?" Ryck asked looking at Vos, who shook his head.

"Unfortunately I was in a bit of a state last night. I must have missed it," he said.

The detective told one of his officers to go and check Vos' phone to confirm the existence of this text. He glanced at his own phone and announced to the room that Lokeren's identity was indeed false. He sighed.

"What a fucking waste of time. You'll be released," he said to Vos, "but you'll be on bail. It's very likely you'll be required for further questioning when the man posing as Lokeren regains consciousness."

The bail formalities took another tedious hour. At the end of it all, Ryck gave his uncle a quick hug and they walked together from the station to the multi-storey.

"Jesus – was I glad to see you, Ryck. But what took you so long?" Ryck explained about his night on the drink, without mentioning Wouters or his grandma. "And what a stroke of genius taking that picture. How come Lokeren didn't notice?" Ryck put on his most nonchalant of looks.

"Oh, it's quite easy to do. I've done it often before – women you know. Now, how about a late breakfast?"

They took their time over the meal. Vos knew he had to tell his nephew about Simone Josse's death.

+ + +

The first thing he saw when he came round was the nurse standing over him, holding a syringe in her left hand. He was instantly in love. His mind seemed to be hovering above the bed, completely detached from the rest of him. He was trying to work out what made her so attractive, what gave her that special aura? He tried to speak but his throat was too dry. He used sign language to ask for a drink. The nurse disappeared from view and he felt bereft. Did she have to leave? He had no idea where he was or why he was there. He had a vague recollection of some sort of collision, something hard and painful. He knew he was Daems and he knew he needed to contact his boss, Rodenbach, but he couldn't recall why.

He drained the glass of water. He wanted another but he didn't want the nurse to leave him again. He held out a hand and amazingly she took it. He had this feeling that he wasn't very good with women. Did he know any nice women? He could bring his mother to mind, but he remembered all too quickly that she thought he was a fool. And he could visualise his spoilt brat of a sister. But he couldn't recall any other women he knew.

He thought about his phone and asked the nurse in a very croaky voice where it was. She told him any belongings he'd had when he was brought in would be in the bedside cabinet. He didn't think he could manoeuvre himself into a position to be able to open the drawer and he asked the nurse if she could tell him what was in there. She opened the drawer and pulled out two items. The first was a police ID card and the second a roll of bank notes. There was no phone. Daems found it all too much to cope with. He needed to sleep.

The nurse left the room and called the police as she'd been instructed.

+ + +

Rodenbach couldn't work out what had happened to Daems. When he'd read in the newspaper about the death of the woman he'd confronted on the beach he'd punched the air. It would save him from any further trouble. He'd phoned Daems but there'd been no response, despite the strict instructions he'd given him to keep his phone on. He'd left a message and had heard nothing since.

He'd just received details of a new 'shipment' – four men who'd be arriving that evening. His contact would confirm the exact location nearer the time. He was instructed to be off the Dutch coast near Vlissingen by 21:00. The transfer of the merchandise would take place about five kilometres out and he'd then sail up the Scheldt to Antwerp. He cursed Daems for going AWOL. He couldn't do the job on his own and he moaned to his girlfriend Sabina about Daems' unreliability. She told him to thank the gods for taking the beach woman and to forget about Daems.

"Look – if you want help why not ask me? I'm not just a pretty face you know and I'm tougher and more reliable than Daems any day. You're such a sexist pig that the thought has never occurred to you!"

Rodenbach was about to launch into a tirade when he realised he was in a bit of a hole. He needed help and he didn't trust anyone else. Sabina had never thrown up on the boat, knew how to navigate and could take care of herself. He swallowed his macho pride and told her to get her oilskins.

The *Leopold* chugged out of Zeebrugge and headed north east. Rodenbach estimated that it would take them between two and three hours to reach the transfer zone. The evening was overcast and there was no moon. There was a slight swell. Sabina took the wheel and adjusted their course slightly having checked the chart. She chewed gum mechanically and scanned the horizon for signs of other craft. A tanker was moving slowly across her field of vision, heading for Rotterdam most likely. No threat there.

They hugged the coast until they sailed into Dutch waters and then headed for the open sea. The wind got up a little. Rodenbach brought Sabina a plastic mug of coffee which she sipped slowly, although it cooled rapidly.

"You see – you don't need Daems. He's a creep anyway. You should see the way he looks at me sometimes. You should get rid of him – especially now the woman's dead."

Rodenbach kissed the nape of her neck but made no comment. The radio crackled. The information was encrypted and he ran the software programme to make it intelligible. He was given a precise location and time for the handover.

"We'll be able to make that OK. Just keep her steady on this bearing."

"I know Leo – I know. I'm the one who's doing the bloody navigation. Why don't you make yourself useful and get me a sandwich?"

He made his way to the small galley. He was not renowned for his sandwich-making skills but at least what he produced was edible. The darkness closed around them. A small cutter passed nearby but didn't show any interest in them and Rodenbach breathed a sigh of relief.

The south-westerly gradually strengthened, which aided their progress, but that didn't stop Rodenbach worrying about the transfer. If the winds were too strong they'd have to postpone the handover. It had happened a few times and Rodenbach hated it. It either meant hanging around with a greater risk of interception or it meant that the whole thing was abandoned, which meant no money. He took over the wheel to give himself something to do. Sabina stood next to him and put her arm around his waist. She knew it didn't do to piss him off completely. The radio burst into life again with a single word – 'lights'. Rodenbach pointed to the switch and Sabina flicked it on and off three times. They saw the response to the north, a little further away than he'd anticipated.

The transfer by rubber dinghy went smoothly. The four Congolese men were safely stowed below deck. A waterproof bag contained four forged Belgian passports and half Rodenbach's payment in cash. He'd get the other half on completion of delivery. The wind strengthened as they headed up the Scheldt estuary against an ebb tide. He saw the lights of Vlissingen to port and then the relative darkness as they moved upstream, passing only small settlements. Terneuzen was a spray of light to starboard but then it was quiet until they headed south into Antwerp. Rodenbach went below deck twice to check on his cargo. The men looked cold, but that was none of his concern. They smoked surreptitiously, cupping their cigarettes in the palms of their hands. One of them asked in French where they were going. He didn't enlighten them about their destination, but made it plain they were to follow his instructions precisely when they docked. He was relieved when they reached Stabroek without incident. Given their port of origin and the route they'd taken, immigration checks weren't mandatory, but Rodenbach had faxed crew and passenger lists to border control in advance – just to be on the safe side.

He manoeuvred the vessel alongside the darkened quay and Sabina climbed the steel ladder and secured the boat. She walked the short distance to a warehouse building and unlocked the small door set inside a pair of double gates. Rodenbach watched from the top of the ladder until her task was complete and then beckoned the four men to follow him to the top of the ladder. The first three made easy work of the climb but the final one missed his footing on the third rung and crashed back onto the deck of the boat. Rodenbach cursed and hoped nobody else had heard the man's shriek. He signalled the three men who'd reached the quayside to move across to the warehouse and watched until they disappeared inside with Sabina. He slid quickly down the ladder and tried to suppress his annoyance at the injured man. He needed

him to move as rapidly as possible. But it was all too clear that the
man had damaged his ankle in the fall. He was overweight and
Rodenbach realised that there was no way he could drag him up
the ladder on his own. Why did it always happen to him?

He made it very clear to the man that he should keep his mouth
firmly shut. He left him in the darkness of the boat and climbed
up once again to the quayside. There was nobody around and
he breathed a sigh of relief. He entered the warehouse building.
Inside was a hive of activity. About thirty men were sorting
waste by hand, separating glass from plastic and newspaper from
cardboard. An all night radio station boomed out over their heads
playing continuous pop music. Sabina interrupted her discussion
with the supervisor.

"Where's the other one, Leo? Don't tell me you've lost him!"

"The bastard's only gone and fallen, hasn't he. I can't get him
up the ladder on my own. I need some help." The supervisor
nodded over to a large man in greasy overalls who looked like he
could pick most men up under one arm. He left with Rodenbach.
Just as they were crossing the quay, a security man complete with
flashlight and a dog straining at the leash rounded the corner.

"What are you guys up to then? A little casual smuggling?"
Rodenbach reached inside his pocket for his cigarettes and offered
them round.

"Just a fag break mate and some fresh air. It gets a bit stuffy in
there," he said, pointing to the warehouse.

"I'm surprised there's enough work for you guys to do a night
shift." The security guard looked as if he didn't really believe
that recycling was all they did in the big shed. Rodenbach was
screwing himself up inside. Would the guy just below them keep
silent? "Of course if there's anything you want to share with me –
I'm your man. Just give me the word."

"I'm afraid the recycling world doesn't generate a whole lot of
excitement. We get the stuff in here and the Chinese take it off our

hands. That's it. All we can offer you is a bale of cardboard if that's your thing."

The guard gave him an I know better look, finished his cigarette and waved them goodbye. The dog lost interest in pulling at his lead and slunk along slowly, tail between its legs. Rodenbach waited until he was certain that the guard was out of sight and wasn't returning and then shinned down the ladder. The big man from the recycling shed moved ponderously after him, obviously not used to this kind of descent. He clattered to the deck, but managed to pick himself up in one piece. He lifted the injured migrant without difficulty and hauled him step by slow step up the ladder. Rodenbach watched from below and then followed.

When he reached the tiny office inside the warehouse, the supervisor started issuing false papers to the new men and instructing them about the job. He spoke slowly in French and the men nodded.

He told them where they'd be living and warned them to keep their heads down. The men looked bewildered, they'd probably had little sleep for days and now had to take in all the detail which would hopefully keep them away from the clutches of the law. They'd paid thousands for the journey and their new jobs and needed to earn money rapidly to repay relatives and money-lenders.

When the shift ended, the four newcomers mingled anonymously with the older hands as they boarded minibuses for the short journey to the hostel. Rodenbach watched as they shuffled off into the grey morning.

He took his supervisor to one side and asked him for the books. The man produced two spreadsheets, one showing the operation of the recycling plant, the other, the costings for the hostel. Rodenbach was satisfied. He knew the plant only just broke even but it provided a perfect processing route for the illegals. In contrast, the hostel was a good little earner, thanks to the high rents which were deducted from their wages before they were paid.

The day shift took over. Rodenbach and Sabina ate breakfast in a small dock-side café before setting sail for Zeebrugge.

Nine

Vos slept for eighteen hours and awoke feeling drowsy and light-headed. Coffee was the first priority, then food. As he sat at the kitchen table he felt slightly more human. He read the texts on his phone. The first was from the police telling him that his alleged victim had regained consciousness. The man could remember very little of his previous life and the police still didn't know his true identity. So Vos was effectively off the hook, at least for the time being.

He was mightily relieved. His night in the cell had brought back all kinds of painful memories and all because of one idiot. His relief kept his annoyance at bay.

Jalloh's text said that of course he'd confirm Vos' whereabouts when Simone Josse had died, but Vos decided not to follow it up. The police hadn't asked again about this and he felt it would be better to let sleeping dogs lie.

He deliberately saved the third text till last. It was from Katerine. She was really worried about him and asked him to call as soon as he could. She was full of apology for not responding earlier, explaining that she'd left her mobile at work. Vos didn't have her landline number and he'd been imagining all sorts of dramatic explanations for her lack of response. He reflected that it was often the most mundane of events which caused real problems. When he called her, he had to leave a message yet again.

His spirits began to lift. As he made scrambled eggs and

poured another coffee, he heard Ryck's scooter arriving, the shed door opening and tools being moved around. This was followed by a very loud whoop of delight. Ryck put his head round the back door and held a phone out in front of him.

"Guess who this belongs to?"

"I've no idea, Ryck. I think you're going to have to enlighten me."

"Listen to this!" Ryck put it onto speakerphone.

"Good news. The woman we've been after has snuffed it in Brussels. I saw it on the TV – nearly spilled my beer. You better get your arse back here, Daems. I need you for the next run."

Vos couldn't work out what the message was all about? Did it refer to Simone Josse and whose was the disembodied voice?

"Can you put me in the picture, Ryck? I have to say I'm totally confused. I mean where did you get the phone from?"

"I found it in the shed. I've been trying to figure out who it was that you slugged, you know, the fake detective. I have to say, I'm impressed by the way you tackled him. I mean I've heard about your reputation but that was way back." Vos looked embarrassed. "Anyway I think the big feller must be this Daems. He must have been waiting for you to come home. You said yourself he looked wet through, so I reckon he must have got fed up of standing in the rain and broken into your shed to get some shelter. I've been telling you for ages that the lock is rubbish. So he waits in there smoking, sitting in your chair."

"Wait a minute – how do you know he was smoking?" Ryck tapped the side of his nose and Vos could see that his nephew was enjoying the intrigue.

"Ah well, I'm glad you asked me that. There was a cigarette butt stamped out on the shed floor, a Gitane. You can tell from the butts and their distinct smell which tends to hang around."

"So that explains it!" Vos cut in.

"Explains what?" Ryck asked.

"I saw this tiny red light in the shed when I arrived home the other night, you know, when Lokeren or Daems or whatever he's called was lying in wait. Then I thought I'd imagined it, but it must have been his cigarette end glowing in the dark." Ryck wondered why his uncle was telling him this. He ignored it and continued his explanation.

"So there is Daems, sitting in your seat in the shed, probably putting his feet up on that stool and the phone slides out of his trouser pocket onto the cushion without him noticing. If it had fallen onto the floor he'd have heard it. I reckon from the way he talked, that the guy who left the message must be Daems' boss. I've had a quick look and there's nothing else of much interest on the phone." Ryck got up and started pacing up and down the kitchen floor. "Maybe he's the one who abducted Simone when she was on the beach."

"You could well be right, Ryck."

"By the way – where's your charger? The battery's nearly flat and I want to be ready in case any other messages come through. They could tell us a bit more about Mr Daems and his boss." Vos fetched the charger from the cupboard drawer and plugged it in. Ryck attached the phone to it and made more coffee.

"So what's our next step?" he asked.

"Ours? You mean mine!" Vos replied.

"Come on admit it, you could do with some help." Ryck was smiling but Vos could tell he was serious.

"My sister would never forgive me if I dragged her only son into one of my hair-brained investigations."

"Come on Harry. I'm nearly thirty for Christ's sake. Just because I still live at home doesn't mean I'm still a kid. I can make my own decisions." Ryck rarely used his uncle's first name, but it slipped out occasionally when he got heated.

"OK, OK. I'll think about it." Vos knew he could do with some help. "Since you ask, I think the next step will be to try and catch this Daems before he's released from hospital and swallowed up by the cops and then try and track down his boss. We've got his mobile number and a friend of mine can get me an address for the owner of the phone."

"That would make things easier," Ryck said. "Listen, I can't help thinking about Simone. If Daems and his boss didn't kill her, then who did?"

"I've been worrying about that," Vos said. "Maybe it was the man who drove Simone away from her house? And where's the damn dog in all this?"

"Dog – what dog?" Ryck looked puzzled and Vos explained about the dog on the beach.

"He belongs to Simone and he's called Barto, but I've no idea where he is now."

"Never mind the dog. Where's the BMW?" Ryck was trying to ignore his uncle's ramblings about some bloody canine. An encounter with an Alsatian when he was ten had put him off dogs. But he was very interested in the bike. Vos looked puzzled.

"What BMW?" he asked.

"When Daems followed me here from Antwerp, he was on a big BMW. I'll bet he was on it when he paid you that visit. So where is it? He can't have taken it with him to the hospital. Maybe it's parked around here somewhere, you know, hidden out of sight. Did the cops mention a bike?" Vos shook his head. "There you go then – it must be here somewhere." Ryck opened the back door and disappeared into the rain.

Vos poured himself another coffee and tipped a generous measure of brandy into it. He was still feeling lightheaded. His phone rang.

"Hi love, it's me. Have they let you go?" All Vos heard was the word 'love'. He rolled it round his mind and liked the feel of it. No-one had said that to him for a long time. He told Katerine he was on the mend and was off the wanted list. She told him she'd be on her way after her final class of the day. He assured her he wasn't going anywhere. No sooner was the call finished than there was the roar of an engine. Through the kitchen window he could see Ryck, helmeted up, on the elusive BMW, moving slowly down the drive. Then he was off down the road, engine racing.

+ + +

People kept asking Daems questions. The nurse asked him questions to test how well his memory was functioning. He could remember his name but he couldn't recall where he lived. He could picture Rodenbach's face and worried that there was something he needed to tell him. In a way he felt pleasantly detached – the less he could recall, the less he had to worry about. He told the nurse very little and somehow knew instinctively not to give her his real name.

He groaned when a police officer walked into his room and sat down beside his hospital bed. The man asked him more questions and slowly wrote down the brief answers, in a large notebook. The man took a dim view of Daems' attempts to impersonate a police officer, and told him that, once he was in a fit state, he'd be charged.

Daems couldn't answer the questions about a man called Vos. He had no recollection of him. When the officer asked him if he wanted to press charges for assault, he replied that if he couldn't remember the man, he could hardly take him to court. He had this nagging feeling that there was another reason why he needed to leave well alone, but it remained stubbornly elusive.

The questioning seemed to take forever but Daems went along with it, as if his temper and frustration had been whisked away along with large chunks of his memory.

He was pleased when the officer eventually left. Answering questions was tiring. He wondered again what he'd done with his phone, although he thought it was probably a good thing that the police hadn't been able to get hold of it.

He leant back on his pillows and closed his eyes. His whole body felt like it was moving slowly up and down, not an unpleasant feeling, just mildly unsettling. There was something familiar about it as if he'd done it many times before.

+ + +

Jalloh stood on the corner of the Rue Alsace-Lorraine. Hardly a minute went by without a passer-by greeting him with a slap on the back or a high five. He was outwardly smiling, talkative, friendly, but inside he was hurting. Simone Josse had been a friend, no, more than that, an inspiration. Why had she died? The papers said the police were searching for a man who'd been seen with her shortly before her death. But the description was vague.

Jalloh worried about who might have been involved in her death, someone with a lot to lose. It was well known that she was on a mission. She didn't like the exploiters, the traffickers, the slum landlords, the employers who paid a pittance. Her frequent court appearances had made her plenty of enemies.

Jalloh asked the people who greeted him, whether they'd heard any whispers. He felt it was his responsibility to find out. The only certain information he had to go on was what Vos had told him – that Simone had been picked up from her house near Geel and driven away. But from the way Vos had described it, she seemed to have travelled willingly.

Most of the people Jalloh spoke to didn't actually live in Matonge. It was too expensive for them, but it was where they came to hang out, drink and eat. He walked on a short distance and stopped on Chaussee de Wavre. He wondered whether he was wasting his time, whether he needed to be more organised in his approach. The sun emerged from behind a bank of dark cloud and he began to feel a little of the warmth of spring. A friend from his student days joined him and they spoke of old times. When the friend dropped his voice. Jalloh could barely hear him. He was talking about the lawyer, the woman, he couldn't recall her name. Jalloh reminded him.

"Yes, yes, Josse, that's her name. She was so good to me. I cannot believe she has gone. I have heard talk going around about a case she was working on. She was upsetting some powerful people who have links with the Durand brothers. Dia – you know Dia?" Jalloh nodded. "Well he went to her house out in the sticks to warn her about the rumours and from what I heard, she insisted on coming back with him to town, said she was getting closer to the top guys." Jalloh was all ears. So it was Dia who brought her to Matonge. He must regret that now.

"Where is Dia, do you know? I need to talk to him." Jalloh tried to control his feelings. His friend glanced at his watch.

"He's probably at Café Nico just now. You might catch him there. Tell him I spoke to you."

Jalloh gave a brief wave and hurried away. At last, something to go on. He headed for the Rue de la Paix, only fleetingly acknowledging friends and acquaintances as he passed. The café was dark, the front window heavily curtained even though it was the middle of the day. The red candles on each table gave off a soft glow and guttered briefly every time a new customer opened the door. A music system at the back of the bar was turned down low, but Jalloh could pick out the unmistakeable sounds of Franco drifting out across the darkened space. His man was in the far corner talking earnestly to an attractive woman in traditional dress. He didn't know Dia well and didn't particularly get on with him. He was one of the hardened politicos, who saw conspiracy in everything. Jalloh had to admit the man was frequently right but it was Dia's preachiness that got up his nose.

"Jalloh – long time no see. To what do I owe your presence?" Not exactly an effusive greeting. Jalloh swallowed his annoyance. It wasn't the time for an argument. Without a word the woman left the table and went behind the bar. There'd been no introductions.

"I'm here about Simone. I understand you brought her here to Matonge." He was trying to be brief but realised he might sound provocative and hurried on. "What I mean is, you might have been one of the last people to see her."

"I probably was, but what are you implying?"

"I'm not implying anything." Jalloh took a deep breath. "Look I'm just trying to get a lead on what might have happened. I mean the cops aren't likely to get far. They'll swamp the place of course, but they'll be easily diverted."

"Tell me about it," Dia said. He was now on his favourite hobby horse which helped divert his personal animosity towards Jalloh. "What do they know? Look, I went out to Geel to warn Simone. It was her who insisted on coming here. I wish I'd refused, but you know what she can be like. Persistent doesn't nearly cover it. I left her at the Centre where she had people to talk to. I don't know who and I don't know anything else that happened. I can tell you though she was getting close to the Durands. I kept warning her that it was a bad move, but she wouldn't listen. I think because she'd survived this long she thought she was invincible. But those shits don't take any notice of reputation or anything else for that matter. Look, how about a coffee? This may take a while. We're on the same page and we shouldn't get distracted by our differences." Dia gave the slightest of gestures to the woman behind the bar and she moved to the coffee machine.

"You'll know about the Durands. They make a lot of money exploiting the brothers and their families back home. Simone was good at digging, good at spotting links. We worked together." He stopped talking and wiped away tears from his eyes. Jalloh was surprised to see him affected emotionally. He'd only ever seen him as the cold, cynical, political operator. The coffees arrived each with a small flower-shaped chocolate balanced on the saucer. The woman seemed concerned by Dia's emotional state, but he waved her away.

"Anyway, what was I saying? Oh yes, the links. They've been clever, built in some insurance. I wouldn't say they're untouchable, but they're well protected. Their only weakness is their cockiness. If they get over-confident, then they could become vulnerable." Dia sipped his coffee. "But how come you're interested in all this, Jalloh? I hadn't got you down as the investigative type." Jalloh wondered whether to tell Dia about the body that Vos and Simone Josse had found on the beach near De Haan. He didn't see that it could do any harm and Dia might have heard something.

"Well I'm already involved with trying to find out about the death of a brother." Jalloh explained as briefly as he could what they knew had happened and what was guesswork.

"And why's this Vos muscling in?"

"You've got it wrong, Dia. This is the guy who found the body. He's trying to make some sense of it all. He didn't have to do anything. He could have just walked away – literally. But he doesn't want to see the killers, whoever they are, get away with it." Dia looked skeptical. "It doesn't really matter what you think about Vos. I just want to know whether you've heard anything."

Dia took his time before he responded, sipping his coffee in a way that annoyed Jalloh. He couldn't have said why exactly. Something about the way he held the cup and took tiny sips, one quickly following the other.

"I did hear something as a matter of fact, but whether it relates to your man or not, I couldn't say." Again he stopped and repeated the sipping. Jalloh had to try really hard to contain his annoyance. "It may be nothing." Another pause, Jalloh almost bursting with frustration. "One of the delivery teams lost a man overboard – an accident they said. It happens now and then. There was no word of a killing. How do you know it was a killing?"

"I don't. Vos suspects it. The skipper from the boat didn't behave like an innocent apparently. Any word on which team?" Dia shook his head.

"That's it man. Now I've got things to do." The discussion was over. Jalloh thanked Dia grudgingly. He eyed the woman up as she came out from behind the bar, carrying a tray of drinks. She was a real looker. Ethiopian he thought.

1993

I'm away for two nights in Leuven, all paid for by my employer De Backer. We're there to find out more about a new air-braking system. The boss thinks we can steal a march on our competitors with this. The guy leading the presentation is German. He used to work for one of the big boys but has since gone out on his own and has a specialist lab somewhere near Essen. He's franchising the use of his system, but keeping it limited. It all seems good to me. We're in a bar just off the main square. The square's full of student bars, all of them heaving, but there's plenty of space here and more our sort of music. I'm keeping it steady. We've got another day of thinking tomorrow, so I want a reasonably clear head.

It's Ben who points her out to me. He's across from England, helping us out with some of the marketing issues. He whispers in my ear that she's been watching me – not directly, but surreptitiously. He dares me to go and say hello. I've had just enough to drink to respond to his challenge. She's medium height, dark hair, nice figure, but the best thing is her manner, not cheeky exactly, but not at all reserved. I buy her a drink and then another. When I finally look back to the table where I'd been sitting with the lads, it's empty. They've gone.

She's called Klaar and suggests we go to a bar where we can dance. I explain about my leg and she tells me to ignore it.

"You'll just have to dance differently. It won't bother me. Come on – let's go."

She leads me out of the bar and into another one. The music is at an ear-splitting volume, but the atmosphere is great, a fun place. She buys more drinks and then we hit the dance floor. She doesn't tire at all and I struggle to keep up. For the slower, smoochy numbers, she's slow and smoochy. Before I know it, we're kissing. This isn't supposed to happen Harry! What about Margriet? What about the kids? I can't hold onto the thought. All I can see and feel is Klaar.

When we eventually leave the bar she pushes me into a taxi. I think it's the end of the evening but she tells the driver where we're going and jumps in. We pull up outside a small, suburban house in a quiet street. She pays the taxi off, fumbles for her keys and pushes me through the front door, putting her finger to my lips. We creep up the stairs into her room and undress. The bed is cold but soon warms up. I surprise myself by how active I am, despite the drink. She whispers in my ear to be quiet as she doesn't want to wake her mother. It's a real passion killer. I sit up, puzzled, wondering exactly where her mother is, but Klaar pulls me back under the bedclothes and we start again.

When I wake, I can't quite remember the exact sequence of the night's events.

Her mother sits at the breakfast table and chats away as if I were a regular visitor. She asks me what I do for a living, where I live and who I live with. I could do without this breakfast interrogation and answer each question with varying degrees of accuracy – motor trade, Gent, divorced and living on my own. Klaar is all smiles and kisses me full on the lips, with her mother there at the table. We leave together and when we part company, we both say we'll phone. I don't know whether either of us means it.

I make it to the hotel just in time for the start of the morning seminar. There's no time for an autopsy on the previous night, just a lot of ribald looks. At lunch I get all the questions. A couple of them have met Margriet, but nobody knows her well. I'm pretty confident nobody will say anything to her. One of them asks about my next date. I laugh it off and tell him it was definitely a one night stand, whilst running Klaar's phone number through my head and wondering where we might meet up next time.

Ten

Ryck parked the big bike behind his uncle's shed. He'd had it up to 150 on one of the deserted back roads and narrowly missed a stray chicken. He took off his helmet and went into the kitchen. His uncle didn't seem to have moved. Ryck hoped he was OK after his police cell ordeal. He had to admit he looked forward to telling all his mates – well, both of them anyway – about his uncle's experiences, suitably embellished and embroidered.

"You insured for that thing?" Vos asked.

"Of course not, but I only went up the lane and I took it steady. I haven't got the confidence to open it up." Vos looked sceptical.

"We'll have to tell the police about the bike."

"Not just yet surely. If they start prying, we can always say we'd only just discovered it. They won't know any different and they probably wouldn't care anyway." Vos let it go.

"Look, Ryck, I'd forgotten. I need to go and find out something about that Wouters guy, you know about your grandma. I don't feel like driving. Will you run me up to that bar this evening?" Ryck had pushed the encounter with Wouters and his grandma to the back of his mind. It really wasn't something he wanted to think about. What could he say?

"I could do of course. But I'm not sure it's really necessary. From what I've heard he's OK. The man can be trusted."

"Who told you that?" Vos was now all ears. Ryck knew he was

being sucked in deeper. There was still time to come out with the full story, but somehow he felt he couldn't.

"Oh, it was the man behind the bar. I had a chat with him about some possible work and we got on to talking about Wouters. The barman seemed to reckon he was a reasonable sort of a guy."

"Well that doesn't exactly sound like a ringing endorsement. No I need to find out for myself, tonight." Ryck wondered how he could arrange to become unavoidably detained that evening. To take his mind off the whole embarrassing subject he asked his uncle about the voicemail on Daems' phone.

"Did you manage to find out anything about who sent it?" The dullness disappeared from Vos' eyes.

"Oh yes, I did. Sorry – I should have mentioned it. My friend Erik, you know, the one in the phone company?" Ryck nodded. "Well he called me back. The phone is registered by a company called LTrading, which is very interesting because a friend of Jalloh's said he thought they might be involved. They're based in Zeebrugge, so I thought maybe we could take a trip down there tomorrow – unless you've got a job on." Ryck was pleased to hear his uncle use the word 'we'. As it happened he did have a job on, but he wasn't going to miss this trip.

"No, I've nothing on tomorrow. Do you fancy going on the bike?" For a moment Vos was tempted. It was years since he'd been on any kind of motorbike. But his leg – his damned leg. He knew it would give him gyp after a few kilometres.

"Sorry Ryck. I don't think I can manage a bike anymore – even as pillion. Can you drive us in my car?"

"Sure," Ryck said. "You know you said about trying to catch Daems at the hospital before he's discharged. Shall we call in there before we set off for Zeebrugge?" Vos agreed.

"I must get moving. By the way, there've been no other messages of any interest on his phone," Ryck continued. "Anyway,

I've got a fence to stain, so I'd better take advantage of this bit of dry weather. How about a nine o'clock start in the morning?"

"Let's make it ten, shall we?" said Vos. "I'm still trying to catch up on my sleep."

Ryck managed to make his exit without any further mention of the Wouters issue. His uncle seemed to have switched his attention to the Zeebrugge trip.

Vos waved half-heartedly as Ryck left on the BMW. He was preoccupied, trying to piece together the story of what had happened since he'd found the body on the beach near De Haan. With a fresh pot of coffee and a ham sandwich smothered with mustard, he jotted down a summary of events and attempted to make sense of it, trying not to let himself be distracted by the birds chasing each other on the gardenfeeder. Was he doing the right thing in pursuing his case, or was he just putting himself – and, more to the point, his nephew – in danger. But he knew deep down that he wouldn't give up until he had at least some of the answers. As he poured himself another coffee, he reflected on how nice the sandwich had tasted. He had a nagging feeling that there was something else he should have asked Ryck, but before he had time to gather his thoughts, his phone rang.

"Patrick's left me again!" No greeting, no small talk, just Kim, his daughter, hitting him full force. "What am I going to do, Dad?"

"And how are you too?"

"Don't get at me when this has just happened. I didn't have to call, you know." Vos couldn't follow the logic of this last comment, but he needed to rewind a little if he was to keep her on the line. Ever since her mother's death Kim had withdrawn from the family for long periods. It didn't help that she lived in London and seldom came back to Belgium.

"Sorry love. When did he go and what set it off this time?" She began to run through the whole story in great detail. Vos found himself looking at his watch every couple of minutes, even though he had nowhere special to go and nothing special to do. Now and then he inserted an 'oh' or a 'right' into his daughter's monologue. He sipped his coffee, glanced at the newspaper headlines and doodled on his notebook. Patrick was, in his view, a waste of space. He claimed to be a musician but Vos had never seen any real evidence of this. Kim worked in the City and was loaded. Vos had no idea of what she actually did and understood less and less when she occasionally tried to enlighten him.

"So, do you think he'll be back?" Vos said, when Kim finally came to a halt.

"I really don't think so this time, Dad." He could hear snuffling over the phone.

"And is there anyone else you might want to spend some time with?" As soon as he said it, he knew it was the wrong thing.

"I'm not looking for anyone else, Dad. I want Patrick. He's the other half of my spirit." The call went on for another twenty minutes and Vos struggled to sound interested. When the call finally finished, he put the phone down on the table and rested his head in his hands. He realised that Kim hadn't asked him a single question about himself.

His children were polar opposites. Eddie, outgoing, positive, optimistic, a real family man and Kim, depressive, a loner who kept the family very much at arm's length. He tried to remember the last time he'd been to visit Kim. He didn't really like going. The visits always started off well but after 24 hours things usually went downhill and he couldn't get away quickly enough. But he could hear Margriet's voice telling him that she was his daughter after all and that he should make more effort.

What was it he'd meant to ask Ryck? He couldn't think clearly. He needed another nap.

+ + +

Daems stood at the front entrance of the hospital. He'd sneaked out for a cigarette, but he decided there and then not to go back in. There was nothing more they could do for him anyway. They'd told him he could expect his memory to improve gradually over time. When they'd asked for a contact address, he'd given them the first one that sprang to mind, a house his brother had lived in a few years back. He wanted to avoid any further interrogation by the police.

As he walked through gates at the hospital entrance, he saw a motorbike speed by and suddenly remembered his own machine, his pride and joy. What the fuck had happened to it? Frustratingly he couldn't bring to mind the registration number, but he could remember every inch of the machine. He fingered the wad of notes in his pocket. The police had asked him where he'd got the money from. He'd told them the truth as far as he could remember it – that he'd earned it and that he always dealt in cash, didn't like banks or credit cards. The police hadn't pushed the matter.

He walked to the train station and stood gazing at the departure board willing it to tell him something about where he should be going. It was unresponsive. He decided that Brussels was as good a bet as anywhere and he'd have plenty of new destination options once he got there. He sat on the top deck of the train and stared out across the fields which were covered in a bright green sheen.

At Brussels Zuid station, he found the bustle hard to cope with and sat on a bench watching passengers coming and going. Then he saw the sea in front of him, boats, a harbour, Rodenbach's face and he knew immediately which train he needed to catch.

Eleven

They didn't actually leave for Zeebrugge until eleven. Vos wasn't even up when Ryck arrived promptly just before ten. He fussed around, showering, shaving and consuming three cups of coffee and two large slices of bread coated in chocolate spread. Sufficiently fortified for the morning, they set off only to return five minutes later because Vos couldn't remember if he'd locked up.

"Let's see if we can catch Daems before he's booted out of the hospital," Ryck said, looking at his uncle, who seemed to take a while to cotton on to what he was saying.

"OK, yes, good idea Ryck," Vos said finally. But their trip to the hospital was a waste of time. The receptionist told them the bare minimum – that the man had discharged himself. No amount of wheedling could get her to divulge any further information about him or where he might have gone.

Vos was seething and moaned about the hospital's lack of help. Ryck remained calm and relaxed and drove steadily via Mechelen and the Brussels ring road, until they hit the E40. He put his foot down and his uncle dozed off, until woken with a start, as they bumped over a pothole on the way into Brugge. They stopped at a small bar on a side street for a generous serving of waterzooi. When they'd finished, Vos cleared their dishes to one side and placed his notebook on the table. He ran through his carefully prepared notes to make sure that his nephew was fully up to date.

Ryck said he thought the key points could have been written on the back of a fag packet, that he didn't need all the detail. Vos ignored him and ploughed on, telling Ryck that they'd start their investigations at the registered office of LTrading and see where that led them.

"Oh, and there's one other thing I need to tell you about. I have a new er…girlfriend." Vos coughed, took a sip of water and continued. "Yes – she's very nice and her name's Katerine." He stopped talking abruptly.

"Well I'm very pleased for you, Uncle. It's good to see you've still got it in you. I look forward to meeting Katerine." Vos muttered something about not knowing when that would be.

The LTrading office was hard to find. Vos didn't believe in satnavs and his street map of Zeebrugge was a little out of date. They eventually located Nord Piersstraat and drove slowly down the street checking off the numbers.

47A was a modern brick-built structure. They parked on the roadside and inspected the building. There were no windows on the ground floor. The front door was flanked by a series of mock-brass nameplates and letterboxes, each bearing a different company name. The box for LTrading was as anonymous as the other five. There was no bell or intercom. They walked round the building, stiff from spending too long in the car. At the rear, were two doors. Vos rang the bell on one but there was no response. He tried the second and, after a wait, an old woman opened up. He asked her about the letterboxes on the front wall.

"Oh, I'm always getting people bothering me about those damn things. They're nothing to do with me, or my neighbour – not that I ever see him. They occasionally come and open the boxes and remove the mail. They're probably all just scams. That's the way of the world these days. Nobody wants to turn an honest franc. Anyway what do you two want? You don't look too suspicious although your shoes could do with a clean."

Vos looked down at his feet and had to agree with her. He took a liking to the woman, who had plenty of spirit, a bit like his mother in a way.

"Oh, LTrading owe us some money and we've come to collect," Vos said. "This is the only address we have. I don't suppose you know any other way of contacting them, do you?"

"That lot are the worst. I've seen a man from there on a large BMW – a K1200 I think it was. Don't look so surprised – my Albert was one for the bikes in his heyday. We used to go all over the place. I still get his bike magazines. Anyway this feller on the BMW, as it happens, I know his mother. I'd rather I didn't know her, but at least I can tell you where she lives if that's any use."

"Yes, that would be most helpful," Vos replied. "Would I be right in thinking the biker is called Daems?"

"You would indeed. Not a man to tangle with and, if I was you, I wouldn't get too close to his mother either." The woman told Vos the address and gave him directions.

"So, does your assistant speak then?" The old woman stared at Ryck who was uncertain how to respond.

"No, he's the muscle in this operation," Vos said picking up on the woman's bantering tone. "I can't do a lot with my dodgy leg."

He thanked the woman and they returned to the car and set off to find Daems' mother.

"Stroke of luck eh!" Ryck said. "Funny how these things work out sometimes. Let's hope his mother's in."

She was. She stood in the doorway of a run-down terraced house near to the station, arms folded, apron tied tightly around her ample bosom. She was all suspicion and didn't take kindly to Vos' opening question.

"You two can bugger off. I wouldn't tell you where he was even if I knew, which I don't. That good-for-nothing hasn't been here for days. He must be off on one of his strops. It'll be Leo, his bloody boss, getting him into something he shouldn't. Mark my words he'll swing for that man. I've told him time and time again but he won't listen, just moons around after that Sabina woman. As if he was in her league! I mean she's too good for bloody Leo, let alone my boy. Stuck up cow though. Anyway I'm telling you nothing so you might as well make yourselves scarce." The door slammed and they looked at each other and burst out laughing.

"Well, we learnt a lot from that! Why don't we have a snoop round the docks area and see who we can talk to?" Vos decided he'd drive. Ryck looked a little worried.

"Are you sure you've had enough shut-eye. We don't want you falling asleep at the wheel." Vos refused to be drawn and slid into the driver's seat.

"Well at least we've got the element of surprise on Daems and his boss," Vos said. "They won't be expecting us."

Twelve

They drove slowly around the docks, having no real idea what they were looking for. Vos assumed that LTrading wouldn't draw attention to itself in bright lights. He pulled in and parked beside a small café which had seen better days. Inside the heating was on full blast and they removed their coats and sat at a small window table. The proprietor wore a long apron which must have originally been white but was now a shade of sludge. They ordered coffees and sipped them slowly. The café was about half full, mainly working men and a couple of youths hunched over their phones. Ryck leaned over and asked a man in overalls at the next table if he'd heard of LTrading. Vos raised his eyebrows at his nephew's direct approach.

"I've not heard of it, mate. But old Willie will know." Noticing Ryck's blank look, the man continued. "You're not from round here then. Everybody knows Willie. You'll find him in the cabin on Zolastraat – selling chips. Have you got some business with this firm?"

"I'm looking for work – heard they might have something going." The man lost interest and returned to his newspaper.

"So, we'd better find that cabin when we've finished here," Ryck said to Vos, looking pleased with himself. They heard the drumming of heavy rain on the café's tin roof and decided to stay for a second coffee.

When the downpour finally stopped, the sky was still dark

with rainclouds and Vos drove with headlights on, peering through the gloom. Zolastraat was just off the harbour road and, as they parked, they spotted the cabin on the corner, with a queue of people waiting to be served. The building had carefully carved woodwork and ornate detailing. The queue moved slowly. When they reached the front Vos ignored his diet yet again and asked for a tray of chips. Ryck bought a large German sausage to go with his chips and squeezed out a small mountain of curry mayonnaise from the large jar on the counter.

"Are you Willie?" Ryck asked the man behind the counter.

"Do me a favour – do I look that old?! No, I'm his son. He'll be on the jetty, just off Kustlaan, with a rod."

They finished their snacks and dumped the polystyrene trays on top of a bin that was already overflowing. Ryck wiped his hands on the back of his trousers. Vos rummaged through his pockets and eventually found a well-used tissue. The sun came out and it was pleasant as they strolled along Kustlaan. A group of anglers clustered on the breakwater, smoking, talking and jostling each other. Vos had generally found anglers to be solitary and morose and was surprised by their levity.

When Vos asked whether Willie was around, one of the anglers pointed to a lone figure about a hundred metres away. That's more like it, Vos thought – a bit of solitude.

"Nice afternoon now. Are you Willie?" Vos asked as they reached the man.

"And who wants to know?" the man said, keeping his gaze firmly on the water. Vos explained about their search for LTrading.

"We'd like a word with Leo, about the chance of any work for my nephew here."

"Have you had any dealings with him before?" Willie looked up from the water and shielded his eyes from the suddenly bright sun. Vos shook his head. "Watch your step then," Willie continued. "He's not the easiest man to deal with. Got a building on the old

fish dock – next to the old smokehouse. His boat's there too – the
Leopold. He was named after the boat, mind, not the other way
round. It was his father's before him, so it's a bit of an age. But it's
a good size – must be twenty metres – and does the job."

"What does he use the boat for?" Ryck couldn't resist asking.

"Oh fishing trips and the like and a bit of other business."
Ryck thought it best not to push his enquiries any further.

"Thanks Willie," he said. "Your chips are very good by the way."

"The best of course! Did you see the silver cup on the shelf at
the back of the cabin?" They shook their heads."

They walked to the car and set off for the fish quay. The outer
harbour was dominated by huge container ships and ferries but
the old fishing port was a haven of smaller boats and warehouses.

"I've been thinking," Ryck said. "Instead of asking him
whether he's got any jobs going, why don't we ask him if we can go
on one of his fishing trips? With a bit of luck, it'll give us a chance
to find out more about him without raising his suspicions. What
are you like on a boat?"

"I've always considered myself to be quite a good sailor," Vos
said, trying to remember the last time he'd been on a boat. "But
that's a good suggestion, Ryck. Just keep the ideas coming. It'll
probably be too late for a trip today, but we could always try for
tomorrow."

They spotted the *Leopold* and guessed the adjacent building
must be the LTrading warehouse. As there was neither bell nor
knocker on the double doors, Vos banged on them with his fist
and waited. The door creaked open. A very attractive woman
asked them bluntly what they wanted. Vos asked if they could
have a word with Leo.

"He's not here. What's your business with him?" Vos explained
that they were interested in a fishing trip.

"The next one's tomorrow afternoon, but it's fully booked."
She clearly didn't have any time for small talk.

"Oh, that's a real shame. You see it's my nephew's birthday and his present from me is a fishing trip. It was a bit of a spur of the moment thing so I haven't actually booked anything and he has to go back to work the day after tomorrow, so this is our only chance really. A friend of mine who knows about these things told me that your trips are the best. Is there any chance you could squeeze two more on board tomorrow?" The woman hesitated. "We can pay extra of course. We'd really appreciate it."

"OK, but it will cost you a hundred each." Vos swallowed. He hadn't expected this kind of price, but then he'd never been out fishing at sea before. "Be here at noon tomorrow and don't be late. We won't wait. You'll need to pay me now."

Vos checked his wallet. He had just over a hundred euros. He glanced at Ryck who took a roll of notes from his pocket, peeled off four fifty euro notes and handed them to the woman.

"I'll need a receipt for that, miss," Ryck said. "It's a lot of money."

She scowled and disappeared into the warehouse, returning a few minutes later with a scrap of paper. Ryck studied it and was about to query something, when Vos stepped in and thanked the woman. As they walked away Ryck asked Vos why he'd intervened.

"Well, we don't want to get off on the wrong foot. We need to keep her sweet. She must be Leo's missus, the stuck up cow as Daems' mother called her – and she wasn't wrong." Vos reached into his wallet. "Here's a hundred. I'll pay you the rest when I find a cash machine. By the way, where do you get all your cash from? The decorating business doesn't pay that well, does it?"

"Not that it's any of your business, Uncle, but I still get lucky on the machines you know and these days they have some big jackpots. Anyway – don't we need to find somewhere to stay tonight?"

1998

The De Backer factory is so quiet. I can hear each drop of water hitting the plastic bucket under that damned hole in the roof. Why the boss doesn't get it fixed I'll never know.

I have to decide what our next step should be. We've been out for four days already. It wasn't as if we'd really planned it like this, but pay has been a big issue for as long as I've worked here. The men have had enough and there's a lot of talk about going over to De Groote's. They're bigger than us, they're hiring and there's a shortage of skilled men – which puts us in a strong position. Except we don't really like De Groote's reputation. They pay better, but apart from that, conditions are poor. Still – it gives us a bargaining chip.

Although I'm not working today, I'm still wearing my overalls – well, my dad's actually. It keeps him close and they fit perfectly – not that overalls are really made to fit. I'm smoking. There seems no harm in it, as all the machines are off.

I glance at my watch again. He's late, like always. The lads are down at the club playing pool, waiting for me to tell them the news. It could be a long wait. Margriet has never really liked me being the shop steward, says it makes me a marked man, but nobody else wants to do it and I think I'm good at it. I won't take any crap but I don't go over the top. I'm not sure the boss sees it quite like that. I have to admit he's done well for himself building the firm up. We've developed a reputation for quality and the boss won't want to risk losing that.

He's here at last. I can hear his bloody Jaguar turning on the gravel outside. He likes the image that having an English car gives him.

"Morning Harry, what have you got for me?" What does that mean? He's the one who should be offering me something. He insisted on this one-to-one meeting, didn't want anyone else from the works committee involved.

"Our claim's already on the table, Bernaert! I need to know your response." Our use of first names doesn't mean a thing. His father was a big landowner and the family goes back years round here. I'm just a peasant and he knows about my criminal past, even if it was decades ago. Mind you I think it helps – the record I mean. Gives me a bit of an edge.

"You can't expect me to respond to that, Harry, be reasonable."

"That's been the problem, we've been too bloody reasonable all these years. We're sticking to our guns now, however long it takes. You know the union's paying us, so you're not going to be able to starve us back to work."

"Now then, Harry, no need for that sort of talk. I am a reasonable man and I'm willing to go to four percent but no more. We'll be uncompetitive if I go any higher and that'll only mean job losses. What do you say? Can we shake on it?"

He's trying to be genial, but I've studied the balance sheet, I know the profits he's making. It's time to play the De Groote card. I tell him what we've got in mind and he doesn't like it, describes it as treachery, a stab in the back of his nice little family firm. But I'm not taken in by his sentimentality.

I move towards the door at the back of the workshop, waving my hand dismissively at him. Just before I reach the door he calls me back. I know we can get what we want now. It'll be just a matter of time.

Thirteen

"You're a dark horse aren't you? You never said that Katerine would be joining us last night." Ryck looked towards his uncle as they walked towards the old fishing port. The first he'd known about it was when she'd surprised them in the hotel bar at midnight.

"I didn't know myself," Vos said. "I texted her earlier in the evening, just to give her an update and the next thing I knew, she was there. Good job you and I already had separate rooms eh!"

"Yes – I did wonder about that – unusual for you to be splashing money around. So she didn't fancy the fishing trip then?"

"Not exactly her idea of fun. Anyway she has to work – but she'll be with us again tonight."

Ryck frequently underestimated his uncle. Just when he thought he'd put him nicely in a box, he'd jump out of it. Still, he reflected, his grandma was just as bad, carrying on with Mr Wouters at her age. He wondered what he was doing wrong. He'd had plenty of girlfriends, but the problem was that none of them lasted. Change of image, change of job, or maybe a car would help.

As they reached the port, the sun was dazzling on the water and Ryck searched in his rucksack for his sunglasses. They saw the *Leopold* up ahead, rocking gently. A man holding a clipboard stood by the cabin.

"That must be him! That must be Leo," Vos whispered to Ryck as they walked up the gangplank. "Looks a bit of a hard case to me, just like poor old Simone said. I wouldn't want to get on the wrong side of him."

Vos felt his phone vibrating in his pocket. It was a text from Jalloh. *LTrading also operate under the name A to Z. Watch your step with them.* Vos showed the text to Ryck, who looked impressed.

They joined ten other would-be sea anglers on the deck of the *Leopold* and stood around waiting for instructions.

"Right, welcome aboard. My name's Rodenbach, but you can call me Captain." A pause, to allow for a ripple of laughter. "We'll have the safety briefing in a moment. Must keep those EU bureaucrats happy." Another pause, but this time, less laughter. "We'll be heading about four kilometres offshore today, fishing for plaice and dab. The forecast is reasonable but we may have a swell later this afternoon. We'll be back here at 18:00 hours. Now for those safety details."

Ryck adjusted his sunglasses and glanced around the boat. It had seen better days, but there didn't seem to be anything obviously amiss. The briefing passed him by. He wondered what kind of paint they used on the railings and then thought about the woman, Rodenbach's woman, hoping she was somewhere below deck. As he speculated idly where he'd take her on a first date, the wheelhouse door opened. Ryck gasped.

"It's that fucking man," Ryck whispered, pulling his baseball cap down lower over his sunglasses.

"Watch your language, Ryck!" Vos couldn't help instinctively playing the father figure. "Which man?"

"Daems, the BMW man, the one you almost killed!" Vos tried to look at the man without appearing to do so. It took him several, sidelong, furtive glances before he was able to confirm Ryck's snap assumption. "We'll have to get off, make some excuse and leave."

Just as Ryck said this, the boat's engine roared into life and they pulled away from the mooring. "Shit, we're trapped. What do we do?"

The boat left the marina and the two of them moved to the back of the boat and stood nervously watching, as they passed the huge container ships moored on the dockside.

"Maybe this wasn't such a good idea. We can't avoid him for the whole trip," Vos said. There was a shout from behind them.

"Come and get your gear sorted out." They both turned to face Daems. He showed not a flicker of recognition. "You need to choose your tackle. Come with me." They exchanged looks of relief.

"You obviously hit him hard. He can't remember a thing," Ryck whispered. Vos hoped the man's memory wouldn't improve at all during the course of the trip.

As they left the sanctuary of the harbour and headed for the open sea, the boat began to respond to the swell. Vos couldn't concentrate on the fishing tackle. He gripped the rail and tried to forget about the large breakfast he'd consumed that morning. Ryck didn't seem to be affected by the boat's movement. He sat in the sun, enjoying the sea breeze. Vos gradually adjusted to the swell and his grip on the rail slackened. They joined the small group of angling novices to receive their initial instructions from Rodenbach. The more experienced punters watched, trying not to look too superior.

The boat came to a halt and the anglers got into position, baited up and dropped their lines over the side. They waited patiently, talking in small groups. Occasionally there'd be a shout and a furious reeling in. Their catch would be unhooked and their trophy placed in a tank of water. Then the small talk would resume. Vos was bored after an hour of no action. He left his rod and ambled across to where Rodenbach was standing, smoking a cigar.

"My nephew seems to be taking to this like…well, I was going to say like a duck to water, but you know what I mean." Talking was clearly an effort for the skipper. He looked briefly at Vos and nodded. He flicked the cigar butt into the sea and seemed about to walk away so Vos spoke again. "Is fishing all you do or have you got other sidelines? I mean, I was just thinking, there must be lots of days when the weather's no good for this." He wasn't going to let Rodenbach go.

"You're right Mr…"

"Harry, just call me Harry."

"Well, Harry, I do have other strings to my bow. I'm a trader, just like my father before me and his father. These days you have to be adaptable and go where the market sends you. You're retired I guess – one of those with a decent pension, no doubt." Vos picked up the challenge in the man's voice.

"I'd say semi-retired, captain. I'm always on the lookout to earn a little extra. In fact I'm a bit of a trader myself, cigarettes mainly. Maybe there's scope for us to do a bit of business."

"Look Harry, I don't know anything about you. You could be retired from the customs service for all I know, on your own kind of fishing expedition perhaps. Besides, all my activity is above board, proper accounts, the lot. You've picked the wrong man. I've got work to do. Daems, hey, Daems!"

Rodenbach turned abruptly and walked across the deck to the wheelhouse. Vos was far from convinced by Rodenbach's refusal to get involved and thought the man might just playing hard to get. Maybe he could try the same approach with the organ grinder's monkey. The wind was getting up and Vos was beginning to feel his insides churning again. He turned down Ryck's offer of a prawn sandwich and decided against returning to his rod. After all, their cover story was that Ryck was the angler. He was just there for the ride. He watched his nephew and could see that he was totally absorbed, seemed to be a natural, using the rod like a professional, each movement smooth and sure. Ryck held up five fingers to show the extent of his catch so far.

Vos made his way over to the wheelhouse. Daems was on his own, sitting reading a girlie magazine. He scowled as Vos tapped on the half-open door.

"Passengers aren't allowed in here!"

"No, I appreciate that. I just wanted a quick word, Mr Daems."

"How do you know my name?"

"Oh, sorry, I just overheard the skipper calling you. You look like a man who knows a good opportunity when he sees one. Between you and me I've got a bit of business to do."

Daems glanced up, checking whether there was anyone close by who might overhear them.

"Come in and close the door – only for a couple of minutes, mind. What sort of business?"

"Ciggies. I need a boat." Vos had phoned a friend of his the previous evening. The friend had dabbled in low level smuggling in the past and between them they'd cooked up a plan. Vos thought it sounded plausible. "Do you ever get chance to take out the *Leopold* – without the skipper?"

Daems was hesitant, weighing up what he had to lose and what to gain. He'd always resented the way Rodenbach treated him as a lackey. This might be a way of getting back at him.

"Yeah, now and then." Daems recalled the only time he'd taken the boat out on his own. Rodenbach had been away and had never found out about the illicit trip. Daems had struggled, even with the help of a friend, but he figured he could manage it again, especially if there was money to be made.

Vos outlined his plan. Daems was hooked.

"It's too dangerous to talk here anymore. Meet me on the harbour side by the boat tonight at eleven. We can sort out the details then." Vos nodded. He was just about to leave the wheelhouse when Daems spoke again.

"I've got this strange feeling that we've met before."

"I don't think that's likely." Vos was trying to keep calm. "This is only the second time I've ever been to Zeebrugge."

"So, where are you from then?"

"Gent – well just outside actually," Vos knew the city quite well and it was his default location for those occasions when he didn't want to reveal the truth.

"I don't know the place," Daems said and instantly lost interest in the subject. "See you tonight then."

Vos closed the wheelhouse door as he left and breathed a sigh of relief. Through the glazed upper section of the door, he could see Daems staring out to sea.

+ + +

Katerine was just starting to make inroads into her seafood platter when Vos announced his plan to impersonate a cigarette smuggler. She told him it sounded like a crazy idea. She placed her fork on the side of her plate and reached for Vos' hand.

"Talk about putting your head into the lion's mouth!" she said. "You can't be serious, love. I think you're getting carried away with this whole thing."

"Look," Vos said, trying to reassure her, "I want to get all the information I can out of Daems, before he regains his memory and before I confront his boss. The smuggling story is just bait to get him interested. I won't be going through with any actual smuggling!" Katerine shook her head.

"If you insist on going ahead with this harebrained idea, then please don't tell me anything more about it. The less I know – the better. And don't tell Ryck about it either. I think you've dragged him in far enough already. "

She resumed her study of the platter in front of her and plotted herself a route via the king prawns and the mussels, to the lobster and the crab in the very centre of the plate. Their conversation stopped.

Ryck arrived bang on nine to drive Katerine back to Antwerp in his uncle's car, before returning to Heist himself. He had a decorating job to do that he couldn't delay any longer, without the risk of losing it. Vos had told his nephew that he wanted to stay on for another day, to see what else he could find out about Rodenbach.

After the pair of them had left, Vos took his time finishing his coffee, sitting out on the terrace at the back of the restaurant, looking up at the stars. It wasn't a cold night. At half past ten he started his walk to the harbour. He thought about Kim and her phone call. Maybe it was time he jumped on the Eurostar again to visit her. As it was hard to prise her away from London, he was the one who'd need to do the travelling.

Vos reached the waterside and walked towards the *Leopold*'s mooring. He worried that Daems might not show, or worse, that Rodenbach might turn up instead of him. When he reached the boat, there was nobody around. He glanced at his watch. He was early. Maybe Daems was hiding somewhere nearby, watching and waiting, to be certain Vos was on his own.

Vos heard a sound behind him. As he turned, he felt a sharp blow to the side of his head and slumped to the ground.

Fourteen

Daems had seen red. As he'd stood behind the electricity substation on the harbour side, waiting for his man to arrive, his memory had come helpfully, if belatedly, to his aid. It had dawned on him that Vos was the man from Heist who'd knocked him unconscious. As he was waiting, he'd convinced himself that Vos was coming back to finish off the job. All the talk about smuggling fags had just been a smokescreen. He'd told himself he'd need to get his retaliation in first.

He realised as he looked at Vos' prone form on the cobbles that he really had no idea what to do next. He glanced nervously around, but there was nobody about. He clutched his new phone tightly and called Rodenbach.

"What do you want, Daems?" Rodenbach was his usual, cheery, welcoming self, Daems thought bitterly.

"It's hard to explain. That man, you know, the one on the boat this afternoon with the nephew or whatever he was. Well it was him!"

"You're making even less sense than usual. What are you talking about?"

"The man who pole-axed me, the same man who went to the Josse woman's house. It just came back to me. I told you – my memory had big gaps in it. Well I've just filled one of them. When I twigged who he was, I must have panicked. I thought he was going to attack me again so I got in first and now he's lying here on the cobbles by the boat."

Rodenbach was about to ask Daems what on earth the two of them were doing at the boat, but decided he had to concentrate on the immediate problem. He could wring the rest of the story out of Daems later.

"Why did you have to knock him unconscious, you idiot? There's no fucking halfway house with you – is there?" Rodenbach ran his hands through his hair. Sabina was waiting for him in bed. He didn't need this aggro. "Look, did he see you before you whacked him?" Daems said he was confident he hadn't been seen. "Well, that's something at least. Have you got the van down there?" Daems said he had. "You'll have to dump him somewhere nice and quiet, but for Christ's sake, make sure it's somewhere where he can come round in his own time. I mean, you don't want another corpse on your hands, do you? And if he comes to before you've dumped him, don't let him see your face. Ring me again when the job's done."

The line went dead and Daems was on his own again. He tried to think. Get Vos in the van – that was his first priority. He ran the short distance to the vehicle, reversed it to the quayside and opened the back doors. It was a hell of a job trying to get the unconscious man into the back of the van, but he managed it and slammed the doors closed, just as a car came down the dock road.

He set off, not knowing where he was going. He realised he was on the Blankenberge road. The beach of course – that would be nice and quiet. But there were those beachside clubs in the town which stayed open all hours, so that was no good. He drove and thought, drove and thought. De Haan, that would be far better, the beach was really long and he wouldn't be disturbed. Then he chuckled to himself as he remembered Rodenbach telling him that was where their missing migrant had washed up. There was something that felt quite right to him about dropping Vos off on the same beach, like going full circle. He kept glancing over his shoulder to the rear of the van to check that Vos hadn't surfaced.

Just south of De Haan, Daems drove down a ramp onto the beach and continued for a further five hundred metres. He pulled his hood up and wrapped his scarf around the lower part of his face, just to be on the safe side.

Vos stirred slightly as Daems manhandled him out of the back of the van and dropped him onto the wet sand. The tide was ebbing so at least he wouldn't drown. Daems' initial enthusiasm for the beach drained away and he began to feel that the shore was a creepy place, the start of all his recent problems. If the migrant hadn't attacked him with that shank, then none of this would be happening and he'd be at home in bed. He closed the van doors and drove back along the wet sand, through the darkness, to the road.

+ + +

When he finally came round, Vos smelt the seaweed that was wrapped around his neck and then felt the gash on his head. At least the blood had dried. His clothes were wet and he shivered. It was just light. He managed to sit up and after a pause, was able to stand. He reached for his phone and was surprised to find it still in his pocket. But it wouldn't work.

He looked around him, gradually piecing together the landscape. As it slowly dawned on him that he was back on the De Haan beach, he felt he was in a dream where the same events repeat over and over but the details change. He'd taken the place of the Congolese man on the beach, except, at least as far as he was aware, he was still alive. He remembered the night before, waiting in the dark, by the boat. He remembered the blow to his head, his hidden assailant. It must have been Daems – nobody else knew he'd be there on the dockside. But why had Daems attacked him, why was he now on this beach and how had he got there? He glanced at his watch but the second hand was stubbornly refusing to move. He needed to get his circulation going. He walked towards the dunes and thought about the bar. Would it be open yet? He emerged on to the track on the far side of the dunes, but was uncertain whether to turn left or right to reach the bar. He went right and walked as briskly as his leg would allow, swinging his arms, trying to get warm. He missed his stick. He was in luck. He saw the bar as he rounded a bend in the track, but as he approached it, he noticed it was still shuttered. He knocked on the door all the same. There was no response and he was about to turn away when he heard the sound of a bolt being pulled back. It was obviously stiff and it took a while before it slid fully back and the door opened. The barman recognised him.

"Well, if it isn't our very own Sherlock Holmes! You're an early bird. We're not open yet, but from the look of you, you're in need of a bit of care and attention. Come on in." He led the way to the larger of the two rooms and offered Vos a seat near the fire which was just beginning to take. "How about some coffee and hot food? While I'm rustling that up, you can have a wash if you like. The sink in the toilet has hot water – we're very civilised here – and I'll bring you a towel. Don't worry if you get blood on it – it's an old one. I hope the other feller came off worse."

Vos followed his instructions. He caught a glimpse of himself in the mirror. His face seemed to have been rearranged by a comedian. He filled the sink and put his face in the water, keeping it there for a while just soaking up the warmth. He washed away some of the blood and tried to avoid touching the scab that had begun to form over the wound. The door to the toilet opened and the barman brought in a towel, a pair of tracksuit bottoms, an old fleece with an advert for De Koninck on the back, some clean underwear and a pair of trainers.

"You might want to get out of those wet clothes. We're about the same size so these should fit OK. Come on through when you're ready."

Vos took his time. Movement was painful. When he was done,

he walked through to the bar and sat by the fire. The barman brought through the coffee and the food and disappeared. He was back ten minutes later.

"So, is there anything else I can do to help? Do you need the police or was it a private matter?" Vos thanked him for his kindness and explained a little of what had happened. "What's the guy's name, the one you think attacked you?" Vos told him.

"Ah, the one and only Mr Guido Daems! He has something of a reputation round here, but his boss is the one you really need to look out for. I used to have a boat myself, did the fishing trips, but I couldn't compete with the likes of Leo Rodenbach. Of course the fishing's just one of his enterprises. He's got business in Antwerp, something to do with recycling and I'm told he owns property there. Word is that not all his businesses are legit and even with the kosher ones, he's allergic to taxes."

"You seem to know a lot about the man."

"Ah, for a while it was a bit of a hobby of mine. I mean he was the main reason I gave up the boat. I'd always fancied getting back at him somehow, but my wife talked me out of it. She's very sensible." Vos thought she sounded like Katerine. Immediately he realised he should ring her.

"Can I use your phone? Mine's full of sea water." The barman handed him a few coins and nodded towards the payphone.

+ + +

As he sat in the taxi, heading back to Zeebrugge, Vos rehearsed what he would say and do to Daems when he caught up with him. The driver kept trying to start a conversation but Vos didn't feel like talking. He paid with his card. The notes in his wallet needed drying out.

His hammering on the door of the terraced house was answered by a familiar figure.

"I'm back for your boy, Mrs Daems, and I'm not in a good mood." He pointed to the wound on his head. To his surprise, her natural truculence vanished and she let him in.

"Guido – get yourself down here now! You've got a visitor." Her voice was like a fog horn. They waited in silence for his arrival. When Daems saw Vos he stared at him open-mouthed.

"What the fuck are you doing here?"

Vos told him exactly why he was there. Daems interrupted, saying that it hadn't been him, that Vos had no proof of anything. His mother scowled and told her son to shut up. She lit a cigarette and stood in the corner, biting her nails. Vos told Daems that he had two choices. He could explain everything to the police or he could talk – about Leo Rodenbach. Mrs Daems spat into the fireplace as she heard the name.

"Guido, don't be a fucking idiot! You've covered for that man time and again. And what have you got out of it? Bugger all. Tell the man what he wants to know and then you'll have to disappear, before Leo gets hold of you." Vos almost felt sorry for Daems. He was a small boy again, being told what to do by his mother. He looked resigned, beaten.

"What do you want to know?"

+ + +

Vos couldn't decide where to visit next – the hospital or Rodenbach's residence. He decided on the latter. His head was throbbing but the pain wasn't as bad as he'd feared. He told Daems to call him a taxi which dropped him off close to the warehouse. Vos wanted to walk the final stretch and clear his head.

When Rodenbach finally responded to Vos' repeated kicking of the warehouse door, he stood blocking the entrance.

"I've come to talk about Moise," Vos said. He was pleased that he'd eventually managed to persuade Daems to reveal the name of the man he'd found on the beach. Rodenbach looked completely thrown. He stood to one side and motioned to Vos to cross the threshold. They sat on a long bench sandwiched between two small wooden dinghies. The place reeked of rotting fish and Vos was glad that, unlike the previous day, he hadn't eaten too much breakfast.

"I knew you were trouble as soon as I clapped eyes on you." Rodenbach lit a cigarette and cupped it in his right hand as if he didn't want anyone to know he was smoking. "You didn't look at all like one of our normal punters. What are you after?"

"I want to know what happened to Moise. I was the one who found him on the beach."

"But there was only a woman there," Rodenbach shouted out, without thinking. Vos looked straight at him and gave the faintest of smiles.

"Do carry on, Mr Rodenbach."

"You may as well know, much good may it do you. I went to the beach to recover the man's body. It's what I had to do."

"Just like you had to threaten Miss Josse, I suppose," said Vos, his voice level. "I think you were behind her death too." Rodenbach held the palms of his hands in the air.

"Look, that was absolutely nothing to do with us. I admit I was a little hard on the woman but that was it. After the incident on the beach, we had nothing more to do with her."

"It's not exactly what your man Daems was telling me only half an hour ago."

Rodenbach leapt up and kicked a plastic bucket full of water across the warehouse floor. The dirty water splashed against the metal sheeting on the far wall.

"I should have realised that that bastard wouldn't be able to keep his mouth shut. I've nothing more to say, so you'd better clear off right now!" But Vos remained sitting.

"Let me tell you what else I know and what I'm going to

do. Then I'll tell you what you're going to do. The first thing is
that I know all about what really happened to Moise. Pinning
a manslaughter charge on you and Daems would probably
be difficult, but I could easily stir the shit up and get the cops
crawling all over this place." Vos looked around the warehouse as
if he could see the police in front of him. "Secondly, I know why
Moise was on your boat. You're a delivery boy aren't you – a bit of
diversification from the fishing?" Rodenbach threw his cigarette
butt onto the bare concrete and ground it with his boot heel. He
paced up and down. A woman's voice called from upstairs, but he
didn't respond.

"You should be very careful with your accusations, Mr Vos.
If you had anything really solid, you'd have already given it to
the police. It looks to me as if you're vulnerable. I mean for a
start, who else knows you're here? People have been known to
disappear." Vos got up and stood right in front of Rodenbach.

"Don't you fucking threaten me!" Vos said in a low growl, "or
I'll hit you as hard as I hit Daems. I lose my cool very quickly – in
fact I've done time for it."

Rodenbach was completely thrown. The man in front of
him didn't look anything like a heavy, but he was menacing
nonetheless. He looked at the gash on Vos' head and weighed up
whether that made the man more vulnerable or more of a threat.
He decided to go along with Vos – for the time being. He sat
down again and lit another cigarette.

"Listen! Moise was an accident. Daems acted in self defence.
But if anyone else started poking their nose in, I'd tell them he
was lost overboard. You claim you found him on the beach and
I know you or that woman called the cops, but if they'd believed
your story they'd have done something about it by now, don't
you think? But of course there's no body and since the good lady
passed away there's no other evidence either."

There was another shout from upstairs and a woman wearing

a dressing gown appeared on the balcony. Vos recognised her from his previous visit. He couldn't catch what she said as she spoke so quickly. Rodenbach said no and she stormed back into one of the upstairs rooms and slammed the door.

"You're right about my lack of hard evidence," Vos said. "But what I do have is an ability to cause you trouble. It's not just Moise's death. A friend of mine told me about A to Z." Rodenbach slumped forward with a pained expression on his face, almost as if Vos had hit him. "Then there's your recycling plant in Antwerp and those apartments. It doesn't take a genius to work out that there might be a connection between these places and the migrants you smuggle in on your boat. You can take your pick whether it would be the tax people, customs or the immigration service who'd be the most interested."

"So what do you want?" Rodenbach had an air of defeat about him.

"I'm after money. It seems to me that the least you can do is to pay back Moise's family for the cost of his ticket. After all, you failed to deliver, so it seems only fair that they should be compensated. Now I don't know what the going rate is, but I reckon that five thousand would be a fair sum. Oh, and on top of that, I think it would be reasonable for me to claim my expenses, so that would be a further five hundred."

Rodenbach couldn't work this man out. One minute he was threatening physical violence and the next he was demanding money.

"You must be out of your mind if you think I'm paying you anything. If I don't deliver, I don't get paid a fucking thing."

"Well it's your choice, Rodenbach. Oh, and you need to know that I'm not the only one in possession of this information. So even if you bump me off, the authorities would still be crawling all over you."

"Christ you're an annoying bastard! I need to think about this." Rodenbach got up and strode out of the door on to the quayside. The door slammed shut and Vos sat waiting, wondering about his own boldness. His comment about the recycling plant and the apartments had been a complete guess, but it had worked. He heard the sound of footsteps descending the stairs and looked up to see Rodenbach's woman approaching him.

"You'll do well to get any money out of him, but if it clears the matter up…" She left her comments unfinished. "I wouldn't push him any further than that though. I've seen what he can do." With that, she climbed back up the stairs.

Vos waited. Fifteen minutes passed and he was just beginning to think that Rodenbach had absconded when the man returned. He went straight to the rear of the building without speaking and slammed the door behind him. After a few minutes he returned with a bundle of notes which he thrust in Vos' face.

"Here's your damn money. What guarantee do I have that this will be the end of the matter?"

"None at all. But to use a phrase you might appreciate, I'm after bigger fish. Our argument is over as far as I'm concerned." Rodenbach stared at him, but said nothing.

Vos walked to his hotel and looked forward to sleeping, despite the fact that it was mid-morning. He was surprised when his phone rang. Could phones dry out? He had difficulty in hearing the caller whose voice was rough and rasping. The man wanted Vos' help in investigating some missing property. The police apparently weren't interested because of insufficient evidence. Vos couldn't tell whether the call was genuine or some kind of wind-up, but he knew he couldn't handle the distraction. He took the man's details and promised to call him back. He was certain he'd never make the call.

2004

I watch the nurse as she goes through the various checks, then straightens the sheets, tops up the water jug and moves to the next bed. Margriet has her eyes closed and her breathing is shallow. I hold her hand and stroke her hair. It's still dark, just a few grey hairs. We've been through all the discussions over the past couple of weeks, from the weather, to the kids, from money which has always been a problem to the car which is on its last legs.

The one thing we haven't really talked about is the cancer. Margriet knows everything there is to know about it. She's read all the booklets, quizzed the doctor, argued with the specialist. And she's told me a lot of this, but I can't take it all in. I felt resentment at first that it should have happened to her. It's lung cancer and she's never smoked. What about those 40-a-day merchants who've never been ill? Why haven't they got it instead of her? I know it's childish but I can't push these thoughts out of my mind. So we don't have a proper discussion. She tells me things, I listen and then find I can't recall any of the detail.

Her eyes open and she smiles at me. I've always loved her smile. Maybe it's the best thing about her, makes me feel happy to be alive. She moistens her lips.

"I don't want to go without saying something that I should have said years ago. I don't want you worrying that you should have told me. I know how guilt can damage a person." She takes a deep breath. "I know about her, about you and Klaar and what happened when you were in Leuven." I don't see this coming at all and I double up as if in pain. How could she have known, I'd been careful and there'd only been that one night. I'd never gone back. "Don't look so troubled, Harry. I forgave you years ago. Your friend Tommy told me. It was eating him up, but I'd guessed anyway. I didn't know who she was of course, but there was just something different about you for a short while. You were sharper,

sprucer, looked at yourself in the mirror which you never normally did."

"Christ, Margriet – I'm sorry. That sounds so inadequate but I don't know what else to say. I was a fool, just the once, but foolish and unfaithful all the same. I should have told you but I tried to bury it, to pretend it hadn't actually happened."

She reaches out and strokes my cheek with the back of her hand. I can't help the tears. I know it should be her crying, not me but I can't stop. She soothes me and tells me over and over that she forgave me years ago. Then she sinks back on the pillow exhausted. We stay there hand in hand as the light fades outside. I can't thank her enough.

Fifteen

The BMW was in Ryck's second lock-up, the one he kept secret. Cans of paint of dubious origin were stacked on metal shelving, alongside a guitar amp that had fallen off the back of a lorry and a hundred household cutlery sets that he'd picked up as bankrupt stock and never got round to selling. He removed the tarp and pushed the heavy bike out onto the rutted forecourt. After locking up, he glanced left and right to check he was on his own and started the powerful engine. It was such a smooth sound – it was clear that Daems had kept the machine in tip-top condition. Ryck rode slowly around the potholes, opening up the throttle as he reached the road. He wanted to hold on to the bike for as long as he could.

He cruised just within the speed limit, not wanting to attract any unwelcome police attention. With no documents for the bike, not to mention his lack of insurance, he was a little vulnerable. He reached his uncle's house and parked the bike in the shed at the rear.

There was one more patch of ground to rotovate – a morning's work at the most. The soil was drier than previously and he was able to make quick progress. Needing a break, he fetched a bottle of lemonade from the fridge and sat on the garden wall watching the passing traffic. He was distracted by a young woman walking towards him, a piece of paper in her hand. He spluttered as some of the fizzy drink went down the wrong way. He didn't know whether it was the long blonde hair, the slim figure or the shapely legs that had first caught his attention, but he knew he needed to speak to her.

"Can I help you, miss? Are you looking for somewhere particular?" It wasn't the greatest chat-up line, but it would do.

"Oh, hi!" He thought her voice was every bit as good as her looks. "Yes I am as a matter of fact. Is this where Mr Vos lives?" Ryck couldn't believe his luck. He could jump straight to stage two.

"He does indeed. I'm afraid he's not in just now but he shouldn't be long. You'd be very welcome to stay until he arrives. I'm Ryck by the way. Could I ask your name?"

"Sure. It's Josina." She looked around at the half-tilled patch of ground and the rotovator balanced against an old apple tree. "Are you Mr Vos' gardener?"

"I suppose you could say that. I'm also his nephew. Do you have business with him?"

"Perhaps I should explain. I've never met Mr Vos before, but I understand he does investigations, you know, missing people, that kind of thing. Is that right?" Ryck told her about his uncle's work and added in a support role for himself. After all, he felt, it was no more than the truth.

"Would you like a drink while you're waiting?"

"Yes thanks. Same as you're having, if that's OK."

Ryck fetched a second bottle and they sat on the garden wall, drinking and chatting. She told him she was from Gent and he wondered why she'd come this far for a PI. She said she worked as a hairdresser and was saving to set up her own business. Ryck thought it was very pleasant talking and was on the point of taking the plunge and asking her if she'd like to go out, when he saw his uncle walking towards the house. He'd been too slow in the build up with Josina, but he hoped he might get another chance later. As Vos drew nearer, Ryck noticed the edge of a white bandage sticking out from under his uncle's hat.

"You haven't been fighting again, have you?" Although Ryck was making a joke of it, he was worried.

"No. I'll tell you all about it later."

"If you'd given me a ring, I'd have picked you up from the station," Ryck said.

"Well it was a nice day and I needed time to think." Vos glanced at the young woman who he assumed was another of Ryck's girlfriends. He said hello and was about to go inside when she spoke to him.

"Mr Vos. I'm sorry to bother you but would it be possible to have a few minutes of your time? It's a private matter. Your nephew has told me a bit about your business."

"Certainly Miss … er?"

"My name's Josina. Would it be alright if we went inside?"

Vos led the way. Ryck stared after the young woman and then returned to his gardening work.

Vos made coffee and found some cake. Once they'd both sat down at the kitchen table, he asked his visitor to tell him what she needed.

"Well Mr Vos. It's a little difficult really. I don't actually want to hire you as a PI. In fact I've had to do some investigations to get myself here in the first place." Vos look puzzled. "Sorry, let me explain. There's really no easy way to say this. My mother is Klaar, from Leuven."

Vos was stunned. Straightaway her face came into his mind. Why was she making contact after all these years and why was she using her daughter as a messenger?

"How did you… I mean… how were you able to find me?" It was difficult to get the words out.

"Well, my mother knew your name of course and for some reason she remembered the name of the firm where you used to work. She said she thought it was in Gent – something you'd said I think. But there was no firm called De Backer in Gent. So I looked further afield and managed to track down their true location, just up the road from here. When I contacted them and asked for your address, not surprisingly they wouldn't give it to me. But I went to the plant and hung around the gates, waiting for the shift to change. I picked on one of the older men as he was leaving and asked him if he knew a worker called Harry Vos. I was in luck. He'd known you vaguely and told me you'd retired a few years previously." Vos wondered where all this was going. What did Klaar want? "I asked the man if he knew how I could make contact with you. He said he didn't know where you lived, but he'd heard that you were some sort of private investigator. After that it wasn't too difficult to track you down and here I am."

Vos poured himself another cup of coffee. He noticed Josina hadn't touched hers.

"So, what is it that Klaar wants after all these years?"

"Well two things happened. Late last year my father died. It was a heart attack." She stopped talking and swallowed. She sipped a little of her cold coffee.

"I'm really sorry to hear that," Vos said. "That must have been very hard for you."

"It was. We were very close. Then a month ago, I became ill. I had to go into hospital for various tests. I had a form to fill in about my health history. There was a section for my parents' health details as well. I started to fill this in and that's when my mother broke the news to me. She'd never breathed a word beforehand. I suppose I can understand why, but it was a huge shock when she told me Dad wasn't actually my dad." Josina took a sip of her coffee.

Vos felt very worried about what Josina was going to reveal next. He tried to stay calm and concentrate on not spilling his coffee. Josina took a moment to compose herself.

"Then Mum told me about you, about you and her, that night, twenty years ago. And, well, I'm …" Her voice cracked and she was unable to continue. Vos sat there, not knowing what to say. The kitchen door opened and Ryck bounced in.

"You two still chatting? It must be a difficult case." When he looked at the pair he realised that something serious had happened. "Oh I'm sorry. I guess now is not a good time. Just wanted to tell you I've finished and I've got to go – work to do. Nice to meet you, Josina. Maybe we can meet up again …er, maybe."

He slunk out of the door. The bike engine was loud as it passed the house, the sound fading as the bike headed off down the road, then silence. It wasn't an awkward silence. They were just deep in their own thoughts. After a while, Vos spoke.

"Well I'm glad you've come, really glad. As you can imagine this is a shock. I had no idea, haven't even spoken to your mother since that night, let alone seen her. Why didn't she…? Sorry that's a daft question. Would you mind if I gave you a hug?"

They stood and moved slowly towards each other. It felt entirely natural and there was no awkwardness or embarrassment. As he looked at her, he saw something of Kim in her eyes.

+ + +

Vos knew he'd have to tell his mother before he told anybody else and that it would be a very difficult conversation. Up until his father's death, she'd been a regular church-goer, a good Catholic. Something fundamental in her had been shaken by his death. She started to question the certainties she'd always taken for granted and as she did so, she mellowed. Vos was aware that she still had her boundaries, but he wasn't sure where these lay any more.

They sat in his mother's front room, normally out of bounds except for weekends and special occasions. They'd played cards together for years, usually on a Thursday evening. It was a bit of a ritual. She would prepare sandwiches and select one of her favourite gins. They played Ecarte for matchsticks, which the winner traded in for cash at the end of the evening. When they broke for something to eat, Vos knew he had to speak up.

"I've got a confession to make, Mother, a serious confession." She stared at him, looking worried. Vos told her about Klaar, about the night twenty years ago, about Margriet's forgiveness on her deathbed. He was surprised that his mother stayed silent and didn't interrupt him until he'd finished. He was even more surprised that she didn't start to scold him, but sat calmly with a serious look on her face.

"So, are you telling me that you and this Klaar are going to get together again, after all these years?"

"No Mother, it's not that. It's more complicated than that." He told her about Josina's visit, told her she had a new grandchild.

"But Harry, what proof is there?" She seemed angry, but not with him. "How do you know the little madam is not just trying it on, in league with her mother? You know – the real father dies, they have to try and find money wherever they can and your name springs up from all those years ago."

Vos wasn't surprised to hear his mother say these things. It was a natural response. He was aware it might sound sentimental, but when he'd looked into Josina's eyes, he'd known she was telling the truth, that she was his daughter and he'd felt a bond straightaway.

"I hear what you say, Mother, but wait till you meet her. You'll see she's part of me."

His mother looked away. She felt her life had changed so much, her husband and Margriet both gone, her own faith evaporated, Kim permanently away in London and now this. It was like something out of one of those TV soaps that she couldn't stand.

"And what do Kim and Eddie have to say about it?"

"I haven't told them yet. I wanted to tell you first."

"Oh well, I suppose that's something I should be grateful for." She looked suddenly sour-faced as if staying calm and reasonable for more than a short period was too difficult for her. Vos was annoyed.

"Come on, Mother, it's difficult I know, but it's hardly the end of the world. It was one night, all those years ago. You'll have to take my word for it and you probably don't want to hear this, but it was the only time I was ever unfaithful to Margriet. I felt guilty for years, in fact I still do, but I can't go back and change things, can I?"

"So, do you see you and this Klaar woman getting back together?

"No! You can't package things up neatly like that. It doesn't work. I only ever met Klaar once. We never saw each other again. And besides, I already have Katerine." It was out of his mouth before he knew it. He hadn't mentioned Katerine to his mother before. Now she'd be all over him with her questions.

Sixteen

Ryck sat at his uncle's kitchen table, spooning strawberry jam on to his breakfast waffles. Vos had been there the previous evening just long enough to shower, change and pack a small bag before he'd set off for Brussels. He'd given Ryck a brief account of his injury and his encounters with Daems and Rodenbach.

Ryck was surprised at what had happened and had told his uncle that he should never have gone to the rendezvous with Daems on his own. Vos had ignored the comment and had seemed pumped up about some news that Jalloh had for him. Ryck had intended to spill the beans about his evening with Mr Wouters, but such was the speed of events that his uncle was out of the door before he'd had the chance.

When the phone rang Ryck had a mouth full of waffle and had to chew and swallow rapidly before he could answer it. It was a woman's voice. She asked for "Mr Vos" and hesitated when Ryck told her he wasn't in. He explained who he was. She sounded reassured and asked if he'd be able to call and see her. She said Miss Josse had been her neighbour.

Ryck finished the pile of waffles and left the washing up piled in the sink. It was about half an hour's ride to the edge of the Kempen. The road was flat, straight and empty and he reached 140 before easing back the throttle and braking before the start of the bends. He pulled the bike up outside the small bungalow, hung his helmet on the handlebars and unzipped his leather jacket. The sun was warming and he stood at the roadside for a few moments before pushing open the gate and walking up the path to the front door.

It was answered by an old woman who was wearing a red headscarf and a matching pinny.

"You do look a little like your uncle. Come on in." She led the way into a snug kitchen kept warm by an old range. There was a small black cat asleep in a basket next to the stove. Ryck smelt the fresh bread and was offered a slice. He helped himself to butter and honey and settled back in a large armchair, feeling that the bread and honey complemented the waffles and jam nicely.

"It's about Miss Josse's house. It's absolutely dreadful what happened to her. Oh I'm sorry – you do know what happened, don't you?" Ryck nodded. "Well, yesterday, there were two men. They pulled up in a large red car. I'm afraid I don't know what sort of car it was. They were in her house about half an hour and then left. I walked across there and looked in through the windows. There was stuff strewn everywhere, tipped out of drawers and cupboards. The place had been ransacked. That's why I phoned Mr Vos. It's very good of you to come instead of him. You see, I remembered then about Miss Josse's mother."

Ryck was surprised. From what his uncle had told him he'd assumed Simone was quite elderly herself..

"She has a mother – I mean one who's still alive?"

"Oh yes. I think she must be over ninety. Miss Josse only mentioned her once and I'd forgotten about it. I don't think her mother goes out at all – more or less housebound. I just think somebody ought to tell her about the house. I wouldn't want it to be broken into again." Ryck finished the bread and sat looking hungrily expectant.

As he tucked into a second slice, he told his host that he'd visit the old lady and put her in the picture. If she wanted some security arranged at her daughter's house, he could do it himself.

Having memorised the directions the woman gave him, he rode along narrower and narrower lanes until he reached a small group of houses clustered around an attractive green. Sheep were grazing there and a flock of geese stood by the edge of a pond talking animatedly to one another. Ryck gazed at the quaintly rustic scene for a few minutes, before tearing himself away and knocking on the door of the end bungalow. It took a while for his knock to be answered. The lady was very small, had a shock of white hair and her skin was mottled and deeply lined. She looked warily at Ryck who explained as quickly as he could why he was there. She shuffled with a zimmer frame and led him into the sitting room.

Ryck offered his condolences and waited while she sniffed into her handkerchief. When she finished, she pushed the hankie up one of the the sleeves of her long grey cardigan. Ryck thought it was safe to move the conversation on. He told her about the break-in at her daughter's house and the neighbour's concerns. He explained what his uncle had been doing and offered his own help. The old lady listened carefully to what he was saying.

"Well thank you, young man. It's nice to see someone of your generation being so helpful. You see so much on the television these days about what young people get up to. I can speak to my neighbour about securing my daughter's house – he's very handy like that. But there is something you could possibly help me with. You see, before my daughter left for Brussels – oh, I so wish she hadn't gone. She'd spent years in Africa you know and come through unscathed, it seems so unfair that her life should have been cut short here in Belgium. Now, where was I?"

"You were going to tell me how I could help you," Ryck said, relieved that he'd kept track of the conversation and not drifted off.

"Oh yes, that's right. Well it's Barto you see."

"Who?"

"Barto, her dog." Ryck recalled his uncle saying something about the dog. "Simone – that's my daughter – brought him here the day before she went off to Brussels. But I can't really manage him these days, can't even take him for a walk. My neighbour has been very helpful, but I don't like to keep asking him, so I wondered whether you could take him, maybe to one of those animal charities."

Ryck wondered if he could overcome his aversion to dogs at least long enough to move Barto to his uncle's house. He asked where the dog was and the woman pointed to the kitchen.

He put his head round the door and saw the dog stretched out on the hearthrug. It didn't stir, looked peaceable enough, long and thin. As he returned to his seat he noticed a small cardboard box on the dresser which held a few CDs. The top one caught his attention.

"I wouldn't have had you down as a fan of Plastic Bertrand!" he said, holding up the CD. The old woman managed a smile.

"Oh no, son, those were my daughter's. She liked all kinds of strange music. She left them here when she brought the dog, asked me to look after them. I don't know why. You're welcome to them."

He looked through the box, but didn't recognise any of the other CDs. They seemed to be mainly classical music he'd never heard of, along with a couple of African Highlife compilations.

"Thanks, I will take them. I lost my Plastic Bertrand CD years ago and my uncle might be interested in the others. Oh, and I think I can help you out with the dog. But I'll have to come back and collect him. I don't know if you noticed, but I came on a motorbike and I can't see the dog riding pillion." The old woman smiled. "So I'll come back tomorrow with my uncle's car, if that's OK." She was clearly delighted and thanked him profusely. Ryck was embarrassed. He put the CDs into his jacket pocket and said his farewells.

He reached 140 again on the return journey and hoped that Daems would never recover the part of his memory that stored the details about his BMW.

+ + +

Katerine gently fingered the wound on the side of Vos' head. When he'd phoned her to tell her about the attack she'd told him he'd only got himself to blame for trying to take on the opposition single-handed. He hadn't disputed the point, but had asked her to join him at his hotel in Brussels. She knew she wouldn't be able to stop him investigating further, but she thought that at least she could try and rein him in.

They lay intertwined, breathless. The sounds of the street filtered up through the partially opened window. Katerine still wasn't sure about what made Vos tick. He displayed an interesting mix of solid domesticity and unpredictability. The more time she spent with him, the less she felt she knew him. But somehow that didn't seem to matter.

She watched Vos as he slept soundly and when his phone rang, she wasn't surprised he didn't stir. She managed to slip out of his arms and took the phone into the bathroom to answer it so as not to disturb him. They'd been expecting a call from Jalloh, but it was Ryck on the line. She explained that his uncle had just gone out, but that she could take a message.

"So where are you?" he asked. She told him. "Well you're not going to believe this." Ryck sounded excited, almost manic. She'd taken an instant liking to Vos' nephew. He showed every emotion instantly and said exactly what he thought, even if this meant putting his foot in it. "You know Plastic Bertrand?" She had a vague memory of a hopelessly catchy Belgian punk song from thirty odd years ago. "Well, I got this CD of his from Simone Josse's mother."

Katerine was already lost and asked him to backtrack and explain about Simone's mother. He sounded impatient, but took her through the detail before continuing.

"When I tried the CD on the player it wouldn't operate. I was really disappointed because Ca Plein Pour Moi was one of my favourite singles." Katerine was lost again – what was he talking about? His voice raced on. "Anyway, it turned out that the reason it wouldn't play is because it isn't actually a music CD at all. On the off chance, I slotted it into my laptop and lo and behold I found that the disc contains not music, but a report – information that Simone must have downloaded from her computer! And guess what it's all about?"

She told him she had no idea. He sounded momentarily disappointed and then sped on. "There's a load of detail about organizations Simone was investigating, hot of the press you know, all about rip-off landlords, dodgy employers, people-smuggling and such like. Some of this is really serious stuff. Maybe that's why she was killed." Ryck's voice faded for a moment, before continuing. "Simone must have been a real dude, digging up this kind of information. Harry really needs to see it. I'll email him all the detail, Kat."

Nobody called her Kat, but she let it go, not wanting to interrupt his flow.

"There's a man Harry might want to track down. He's active in an organization which Simone calls the Group. Most of their activity looks above board, but they've got sort of undercover operation as well which seems to be this man's speciality. But more important for Harry, he's got a link with Zeebrugge. Wait a minute I'll just check. He's got some sort of code name – First Base, that's it."

"What did you say just then, Ryck?" Katerine managed to keep her voice level.

"Er…First Base. It doesn't say what his real name is. Oh, and before I forget, tell Harry he's inherited a dog. I'll explain when he gets back."

With that, the whirlwind was gone. Katerine stayed in the bathroom trying to calm her nerves. Christ, how had this happened? She crept back into the bedroom, replaced the phone on the bedside table and lay down beside Vos, her breathing still too rapid. He stirred slightly and started snoring. She nudged him gently and he fell silent. She watched the curtains blowing, felt suddenly cold and pulled the duvet up around her shoulders. She tried to push First Base to the back of her mind.

+ + +

When Ryck's email arrived on the phone, she still didn't wake Vos. She scanned the attachment rapidly. Simone Josse had been very thorough in her research. Katerine, searched for any detail that might compromise her. There was nothing that looked potentially incriminating. She lay still, one hand clasping her throat, while the other twisted a small silver bracelet round and round her wrist. She wondered what exactly she should tell Vos – and when.

She woke him gently. He kissed her and pulled her towards him. Later he read Ryck's email while she sat silently on the edge of the bed.

Seventeen

Tys Hendrickx pushed his fingers between two of the slats on the venetian blinds and prised open a gap just wide enough to see what the weather was doing. He decided he could leave his umbrella behind. He peered down to the street, three floors below. He switched the phone from his left to his right ear and walked across the thickly carpeted room to the mirror above the drinks cabinet. He fingered his goatee as he checked his appearance, a lean face, close cropped hair, rimless glasses and that single grey hair nestling in the beard.

"As I told you before, it should never have happened. You need to get your act together Rodenbach." He was calmly threatening. "Don't forget, you're not the only contractor I can use. And remember – this is going to cost you!" He finished the call.

His office was out of bounds to anyone, bar one or two trusted employees. He handled the sensitive business. The activities on the two floors below were above suspicion, regular, civic-minded even. He finished his brandy and replaced the glass on a small wooden tray. He didn't like loose ends. He'd used Rodenbach for a number of years without problems – up until now. But he was at a disadvantage. Despite his comment on the phone, there wasn't anybody else who could immediately step into the breach and Rodenbach had the advantage of providing an integrated service, moving migrants that crucial last step, employing them and housing them. Still – he couldn't ignore a dead man, even if, as

Rodenbach had told him, he'd been disposed of safely. But maybe it gave him some leverage which he could exploit profitably.

He told his PA he was leaving and took the private lift down to the ground floor. It was small and cramped and he was relieved to emerge into the dark, narrow lobby below. He pushed open the fire door, stepped out into the street and watched the door as it slammed shut. He looked up at the five storey 1960's building. Its grey, anonymous exterior gave nothing away. He pulled up the collar of his long black overcoat and set off for lunch.

+ + +

As they sat on the back seat of the taxi, Vos studied the streetmap to double-check the location of the restaurant highlighted in red. Jalloh had given him the map and told him the 'big fish' that Vos was after was a regular there. Of course there was no guarantee that he'd put in an appearance, but with Katerine by his side, Vos felt lucky – not that he really believed in luck. He'd go as far as 'the right place at the right time' and conceded there might be an element of luck in that. But in his view, that was usually down to good planning.

"So, run that past me again – about the amulet," he said. Katerine looked pleased with herself.

"Well it's really all down to J. You remember there were a few words on Moise's amulet in a local dialect. J identified this as Lunda Kambove. Kambove's in the south of Katanga Province and that's where I'm going to concentrate my search. If I could find out his surname, then I'd have a better chance of tracking down his family."

"It's a real shame I couldn't get it out of Rodenbach." Vos said. "He claimed he didn't know Moise's real surname – only the one on his forged passport."

"Never mind love. We'll get there."

They sat close together, talking in low voices. The taxi driver eyed the couple through his rear view mirror, watched as they talked, smiled and moved closer together. He wondered what they were on and thought that whatever it was, he could do with some. When Vos signalled, the driver stopped. They were a short distance from the restaurant.

As they walked arm in arm alongside the Canal de Charleroi, Vos told her how surprised he'd been when Rodenbach had handed over the compensation money for Moise's family. But then perhaps the man wasn't as hard as he looked. Vos thought that money would be better than nothing and he knew there'd be no chance of police action over Moise's death – no body, no forensic evidence and, very conveniently, no longer any witnesses who'd have any credibility in countering Rodenbach's version of events.

When he'd succeeded in getting the compensation Vos had thought about calling it a day. But then a small voice had told him to keep going, to try and find one of the bosses and to let them know that he knew what they were up to.

They turned away from the canal bank into a side street. Traffic was heavy, noisy and slow moving, with vehicles double-parked, loading and unloading. They stepped around a crate of live chickens, their heads bobbing in and out of their temporary prison. Vos liked the bustle, the liveliness of the place. He couldn't see himself living in the city, but for the moment he felt a buzz. Katerine seemed preoccupied, not her usual lively self.

Vos' phone rang. The rough voice seemed familiar.

"Mr Vos. I called before but you haven't been in touch. It's about that missing property I mentioned. I need to know whether you can do anything or not. It's getting urgent." Vos tried and failed to recall the details.

"Look, I'm sorry you'll have to forgive me. I've been very busy since you called." Vos had to make a quick decision. Tell the man he couldn't help or take him seriously? "Yes I can help you. Where do you want to meet?" The man gave him the address of a bar in Heist. "I know it," Vos said. "How about next Tuesday at six?" The caller agreed. Vos thought he sounded disappointed that it wasn't sooner.

Somebody with a wry sense of humour had named the restaurant 'Heart of Darkness'. The place lived up to its name and the large basement room was lit solely by candles. The intricate wax sculpture in one corner caught Vos' eye. He flipped a coin into the bucket and placed a new candle at the side of the structure, the start of a breakaway development perhaps. He wondered what happened to the coins.

They found a table only just big enough for two, with a good view of the entrance and studied the menu. It wasn't cheap. Their drinks arrived, fruit concoctions in tall glasses, complete with swizzlesticks and tiny pink umbrellas. Vos pulled a photo that Jalloh had given him from his inside pocket and peered at it again just to remind himself of what Hendrickx looked like. He showed it to Katerine and she nodded, then gestured for him to put it away. He surveyed the room without trying to look too obvious but there was no sign of the man. Their tapas starters arrived, and they ate slowly, holding hands under the table. When he'd finished, Vos went downstairs to the toilet. He returned looking particularly animated.

"He's downstairs," he whispered.

"What do you mean downstairs?"

"There's another dining area down there – as well as the toilets. He's sitting with another man and from the way they're talking and gesturing, I don't think they're just business acquaintances." Vos raised his eyebrows. "They're just starting their mains. I think they'll be a while yet, so we've no need to rush."

Katerine seemed concerned by the news, even less relaxed than she'd been previously.

The sea bass was excellent, well worth the price, Vos thought. He suggested they skipped the dessert course so they could be ready to leave at very short notice. Katerine paid and they lingered over their coffees. Vos almost missed the two men when they eventually emerged from the lower room and made their way up the stairs to the entrance.

He and Katerine followed them outside at a distance. At the first street corner, Hendrickx embraced his companion and watched him walk away towards the metro station. He flicked something off his right shoulder, put on a pair of leather gloves and set off at a brisk pace in the opposite direction.

Vos struggled to keep up. He was having a bad leg day. They waited at the pedestrian crossing for the light to go green.

"Are you OK, Harry?"

"It's just the leg. I'll be fine." Hendrickx was pulling further away from them.

"We don't want to lose him," Katerine shouted to make herself heard above the traffic. "Look, I'm going to run ahead and keep him in sight. I'll keep my phone on so you can check where I am."

"You can't go after him on your own – it's too dangerous." Vos was exasperated and alarmed in equal measure, but she was having none of his caution. She kissed him on the cheek and streaked away. He stood in the middle of the pavement with his arms spread out, shouting her name.

"Get out of the way, old man!" Vos realised he was blocking the street and stood to one side to let an annoyed-looking teenager pass by. He pulled out his phone, but the call went straight to voicemail.

+ + +

Katerine watched Hendrickx from a distance, as he bought an ice cream from an Italian gelateria and walked on at a slower pace, juggling phone and cornet. After a few minutes Hendrickx disappeared into the Hotel Magritte. Katerine followed him inside. He sat down on a large, leather sofa in the foyer and ordered a drink from a passing waiter.

"Do you mind if I join you, Mr Hendrickx?" The woman sat down in the armchair opposite him. It took him a moment for him to focus. He'd dropped a small blob of ice cream on his tie and was preoccupied with removing it.

"Who the fuck are you?" he said.

"I'm Bookworm."

"What did you say?" She repeated herself and he stared at her, completely thrown.

"But you're a woman!" was all he could think of saying.

"That's the beauty of emails – they're sexless. So you're 'First Base'. Somehow I'd pictured a younger man." He ignored her comment.

"Look, if you're Bookworm, you'll know the rules. There's not supposed to be any face to face contact."

"This is different. You're about to be exposed. Can you get me a drink – a prosecco?" Hendrickx signalled to the waiter.

They sat uneasily until the drink arrived. She took a sip and continued to hold the glass in her hand, seemingly reluctant to set it down on the table. She told him about the body on the beach near De Haan, about the man and the woman who'd found the body and about the man called Rodenbach who taken the body away.

"And why should this be of any interest to me?" Hendrickx asked, almost dismissively.

"Because I'm ninety-nine percent certain that you commissioned Rodenbach and that means you're compromised. The man who found the body is after you. He knows your name, he's here in the city right now and he wants to expose you. The thing I can't understand though is what the hell happened to the woman on the beach, Simone Josse. Why did she have to die?

Surely that puts an end to everything the Group's built up so carefully. When they finally get their arses into gear, the cops will be crawling all over us."

"That's where you're wrong er…what's your real name? I can't keep calling you Bookworm."

"It's Katerine."

"Well Katerine, let me tell you that her death had absolutely nothing to do with us. She died of a heart attack. The news will be released very soon."

"That's unbelievably convenient isn't it? Where did your information come from?" Katerine was highly sceptical, but she hoped, she really hoped that Hendrickx was right.

"I didn't believe it at first either. But my source is reliable – very reliable. Apparently the old girl had a dicky heart for years, but ignored all the medical advice. It all went wrong for us because our guy who was with her when she keeled over panicked. If he'd just called an ambulance he'd have been OK, but it wasn't clever to do a runner and to leave his belongings strewn around the room. Still I think we can get him out of it, now the medical evidence is there. Anyway enough of that, what about this guy who wants to nail me? How come you know him?"

Katerine hesitated and felt her face reddening.

"Oh shit – don't tell me you're sleeping with the enemy!"

How had he guessed? Was she so transparent? Katerine took a deep breath and tried to compose herself.

"It's a good thing I am, otherwise he'd be sitting here now and you'd be finished. I know what he's like. He's pieced this whole story together."

"So how do we stop him?"

"I'm going to tell him the truth."

"What – are you out of your mind?" Hendrickx realised he was shouting and looked warily around the hotel foyer. But nobody seemed to have noticed. He dropped his voice. "Look, what do you really know about the man, apart from what he's like in bed – next to nothing I'd bet." She didn't rise to the provocation.

"You want to be careful, Mr Hendrickx. You need me. I know how the man ticks and he'll listen to me." He saw the sense in what she was saying.

"OK, so you talk to him and tell him why we do what we do. Is that it? Will that be enough to call him off?

"Yes – that and a five grand payment."

"You didn't tell me he was in it for the money. From what you said I assumed he was just an interfering busybody."

She told him about the five thousand her man had squeezed out of Rodenbach, about how it would be only sufficient to allow the dead man's family to pay off the money-lenders.

"Another five grand will help to compensate the family for loss of earnings – a small gesture don't you think?" She ordered another prosecco and glanced at her phone – three messages from Vos already. He'd be climbing the walls, but she didn't want to be interrupted yet.

"I suppose you think I'm going to hand this money over – just like that?"

"Of course – you don't have a lot of choice really." He sat brooding, ill at ease. This was all Rodenbach's mess. But then he didn't want the mess to get any worse, especially with the new business he had in mind. He shrugged his shoulders.

"I'll give you the money. We need to draw a line under this. What happens to Bookworm now? Are you pulling out?"

"No, no, we carry on as before – once you've handed the money over."

+ + +

Ryck had to admit he was a complete beginner when it came to dogs. He'd been to the library and borrowed a large book on pet care. He opened this out on the kitchen table in his mother's house and leafed through the pages slowly. Barto lay in his new basket, next to the two shiny new bowls.

Ryck's mother had taken some persuading to allow the dog in the house, even on a temporary basis. She feared she'd end up being lumbered with it. Ryck in contrast was confident his uncle would jump at the chance of a free dog, already house-trained, good for walking and pleasant company.

His phone rang. It was his uncle Pieter.

"Hello Ryck. I wanted Harry but he's not answering. I need some help. Can you come over?" Ryck hadn't seen Pieter for a good while.

"Do you like dogs, Pieter?"

"What kind of dog?"

"I'll show you. I'll bring him over. I'll be about thirty minutes."

As he drove over to the Kempen, with the dog stretched across the back seat of Vos' car, Ryck remembered Harry telling him about Pieter when he still lived in the big hospital. He shuddered at Harry's description of the place, the large bleak wards, the overpowering smells of urine and stale food and the undercurrent of fear.

Ryck parked in the driveway of the large bungalow and let Barto out. The dog sniffed around and then waited by the front door. It was opened by one of Pieter's housemates who showed them into the large living room at the front of the house. It had a view out over the marshlands. There was a pair of binoculars on the window sill. Pieter came slowly into the room. He moved in a very deliberate manner and shook hands with Ryck.

"What's his name?" Pieter asked, pointing to the dog.

"Barto. He belonged to an old lady who died recently and I'm hoping Harry is going to look after him."

"He could live here," Pieter said. "We'd all have to agree, but I'm sure we would."

"You'd have to ask the house manager wouldn't you?"

"Yes, we'll ask him. I phoned Harry to tell him something." Pieter looked around the room to double-check there was nobody else there. "I've got a girlfriend."

"That's good, Pieter. When did this happen?"

"Oh, it was last week. I want to visit Harry and bring my girlfriend."

"I'm sure he'll be pleased to see you both. I'm not sure exactly when he'll be back. He's in Brussels on some business. I'll ask him to ring you when he comes home. How about we take the dog for a walk?"

They set off along a footpath that wound its way through the marshes. Ryck took the binoculars with him and stopped periodically to watch the birds gathered at the edge of the water. Pieter held the dog lead tightly and moved ahead of Ryck. They reached a small cabin which sold drinks and snacks to the walkers and bird watchers. They sat on the wooden bench and drank coffee out of plastic beakers. Pieter told a story which Ryck had heard before, about a family visit to the seaside when he was a boy. They'd all been there, his mum and dad, Harry and Ryck's mum. Pieter described the funfair and the ride on the big dipper, the wind whistling through his hair.

+ + +

Vos stared at his phone, willing it to ring, but it remained stubbornly mute. Katerine had been gone for an hour and he'd heard nothing from her. He wondered whether he should call the police. He cursed his damn leg again.

He sat at an outside table of a side street cafe, eking out his coffee. Although it had long since gone cold, he sipped at it now and then, trying to maintain the pretence that he was just another tourist. He glanced at the newspaper. The headline on the front page was about another government crisis which seemed remarkably similar to the previous one. He pretended to study the league tables on the back page, but, unlike his son Eddie, he'd never really taken much interest in football. He couldn't recall whether it was unusual for Anderlecht to be top.

When his phone finally rang it startled him and he dropped his coffee cup, the cold dregs spraying across the table and onto his trousers.

"Shit! Oh sorry, not you love. I've just spilt my coffee all over the place. Where have you been? I've been worried sick."

"You poor thing! I'm fine and I've got a lot to tell you. Where are you?" Vos was unsettled by her tone of voice. She sounded like she was putting on a front. "Actually it doesn't matter where you are. Why don't we meet up at the hotel? I'll get a taxi there. Can you do the same?"

Vos agreed, but he felt uneasy. He paid for his coffee and asked the barman if he could get him a taxi. It took a while to arrive. As he sat in the back seat he replayed his last conversation with Katerine. It didn't feel right, something had changed. The driver stopped abruptly in the middle of the street and wound down his window.

"I won't be a moment, sir. I just have to speak to my friend here." Vos had no idea what language they were speaking, but their discussion went on and on. Vos asked the driver how much longer they'd be. "Only a moment, just a moment, sir."

Vos heard his phone ring again. It was Ryck

"I'm at the hospital. You need to come, Harry. It's Grandma."

+ + +

Ryck had never liked hospitals, the smell of illness lurking behind the antiseptic. The light from the fluorescents bounced off the over-polished floor, but Ryck felt it would be inappropriate to put on his sunglasses. He couldn't face another visit to the drinks machine. There were already three half-emptied cups lined up in front of him on the low table. He flicked through the dog-eared magazines again, but they were of no more interest than they had been first time round.

Mr Wouters was pacing the corridor. Ryck had been pleased to see him arrive an hour ago, pleased that his interest in Grandma extended to hospital visiting. Ryck felt that he deserved being moved up a notch or two on the 'how much to trust you' scale. But they'd run out of things to talk about and the silence of sitting together had proved too awkward. Ryck tried to estimate his uncle's likely arrival time. It would depend, of course, on taxi availability at both ends of the journey, but he reckoned on another ten minutes.

A tall man in a white coat swept into the waiting area and asked for Mr Vos. Ryck looked up.

"You can go in now if you like, but don't stay too long." Ryck asked about the other visitor. "Well maybe five minutes each. We don't want to tire her, do we?"

Ryck explained the arrangements to Mr Wouters as he passed him in the corridor and went into the room where his grandma was lying very still. He sat on the chair and tried to think of something to say. His mind went blank. He didn't really know how ill she was. The man in the white coat hadn't said much on that score and Ryck felt that he was probably waiting for Harry to arrive before going into more detail. Without opening her eyes, or moving at all, she asked Ryck if he was OK. He felt he should be the one asking her. He started talking about his day, about Pieter and Barto the dog and the walk they'd been on. His grandma asked him about what he'd seen, what the dog was like and where it had come from. Before he knew it, his five minutes were up and he was handing the visiting baton on to Mr Wouters, who seemed completely at home sitting at the patient's bedside, his first words soothing and quietly confident.

Ryck almost collided with his uncle in the corridor.

"Mr Wouters is in there just now," he said.

"Who?"

"You know," Ryck said awkwardly. "Grandma's gentleman friend." Vos looked annoyed.

"What on earth's he doing here?" Ryck explained as calmly as he could and asked his uncle just to wait for a few minutes. Vos looked put out and kept glancing through the glass panel in the door to the room where his mother lay.

"Give the man a bit of privacy, won't you!" It came out sharper than Ryck had intended, but he felt annoyed by his uncle's petulance.

"I've raced here from Brussels and now I'm having to wait for a man who has only known her for five minutes." He fidgeted in his corner seat. A few minutes later Wouters emerged from the room and walked across to Vos. He introduced himself and held out his hand. There was an uncomfortable moment when Ryck thought his uncle was going to refuse to shake hands, but the moment passed. Vos mumbled something inaudible to the old man and went into his mother's room.

As soon as he sat on the plastic bedside chair, Vos thought of his wife's last few days. It was the same hospital, on the same floor, but thankfully a different room. There were two get well cards on the bedside cabinet, a bowl of fruit and a plastic jug of water with two plastic mugs. Vos poured himself some water and sipped it slowly.

"So, you're here at last Harry. Where've you been?" She looked drawn but he supposed that was only to be expected. He wondered how much to tell her.

"I've had some business in Brussels. Sorry, it took a while to get a train. Anyway how are you? Ryck tells me you fainted again."

She went through a long description of the events of her day, the fall, coming round on the floor, being unable to move, her shock on hearing the front door creaking open and the relief of seeing her neighbour in the living room doorway, spare key in hand.

Vos' phone beeped, but he ignored it, knowing it would be Katerine and not wanting to be distracted. There was a light tap on the door and a tall, thin man breezed into the room, introducing himself as Mrs Vos' consultant. Vos shook hands with him and confirmed he was the patient's son. The consultant spoke slowly, making sure that Mrs Vos was following him, as he explained that it would not be safe for her to continue living on her own. She'd known deep down that this was coming. She hadn't told her son the full extent of her problems, but she'd told the consultant, hoping that he'd be able to come up with a magical medical solution. As he left the room, the consultant asked them to have a think about the best way forward.

They sat silently for a while, each consumed by their separate fears. But it was really the same fear, the loss of independence. Vos made his decision.

"You'll have to come and live with me, Mother. I'm afraid your house isn't suitable for you anymore and Sis would only have space if Ryck moved out – and I can't see that happening anytime soon. I'll have to get help in of course, but it's the only way forward." As he spoke, he thought of the problems, their basic incompatibility, the arguments, the silences and the slowly simmering atmosphere that would hang over the house.

He turned to listen to what his mother had to say, but she had fallen asleep.

Eighteen

Daems knew he had to escape. Rodenbach would be after his blood – maybe literally. He'd left Zeebrugge in a hurry and headed for Brussels. There he felt he'd have more chance of being anonymous, biding his time, trying to stay out of harm's way. He was immediately at home in the small run-down hotel near the Zuid Station. He slept a lot, watched TV, ate in the Moroccan café across the road and drank in the tiny hotel bar. So far there'd been no sign of Rodenbach, but Daems worried that his boss might not be able to resist the temptation to track him down. As he lay on the bed, tossing the TV remote from one hand to the other, he had a sudden vision of his beloved BMW parked up behind a large garden shed. The medics had been right. His memory was continuing its recovery, but it was taking longer than he'd expected. He concentrated hard, trying to bring to mind the location of the shed. Then it clicked – the man on the boat, the man who'd hit him and put him in hospital, the man who was the source of all his recent troubles. It was his shed. Now all he had to do was remember where the man lived.

+ + +

Ryck put a spadeful of soil into the riddle and shook it vigorously, watching the fine grains emerging into a heap on the ground. Although the work was repetitive he enjoyed it.

He regretted not having asked Josina out, when he'd had the chance. Harry had given nothing away about his discussion with her and had muttered something about client confidentiality. Ryck had known from his uncle's body language that there'd been more to it than that.

He wheeled the barrow over to the compost heap, filled it and pushed the heavy load back to the trench he'd already dug. As he took a forkful of the decayed vegetation from the barrow, he glanced up and saw a man moving furtively towards the garden shed. Ryck hid behind one of the apple trees and watched as the man peered in through the shed window. Once he got a clear view of him, Ryck realised it was Daems. The man must have finally remembered where he'd left his bike.

"Oi – what are you up to?" he shouted across the garden. Daems jerked his head round and saw Ryck.

"I've come for my fucking bike. Why do you think I'm here?"

"OK, calm down and I'll let you in." Ryck walked across the garden towards the shed. "You should be thanking me! I've been looking after it for you, waiting for you to return. I knew you'd be back – nice bike like that." He reached the shed and looked Daems up and down. "You OK? You look a bit under the weather?"

"Never mind what I look like – just unlock the bloody door."

Ryck pulled a key from his jeans pocket. He opened the shed door and gestured for Daems to go in. A soon as the man was inside, Ryck slammed the door shut, locked it and put the rarely-used metal security bar in place. Ignoring the shouts and curses, he went to the house and put the kettle on.

Half an hour later he returned to the shed.

"I see you've calmed down, Mr Daems. Quite nice in there, isn't it?" He was answered with a violent hammering on the door. "Look, I'll let you out once you tell me what really happened on that boat. How did Moise die?" There was silence.

Daems was worn out. He just wanted to get on his bike and leave everything else behind, Rodenbach, his mother, his past and the annoying bastard outside. What had he got to lose if he told the lad what had happened? After all it had been, more or less, an accident.

"OK son, you've got a deal. Just let me out and I'll tell you." He sounded weary. Ryck knew he had the upper hand.

"You must be joking.! You're not going anywhere until you tell me. The sooner you start talking, the sooner you can leave." There was silence again and then Daems started to tell him the whole story.

+ + +

Ryck watched as the BMW sped off. He really was sorry to see the bike go. Daems had gone for him when he'd finally opened the shed door, but Ryck had been ready. He'd been pleasantly surprised that he'd been able to put the lessons from his self-defence classes all those years ago to good use. But he knew he'd been lucky that an unfit Daems had only been operating at about half power. He couldn't wait to tell his uncle what he'd managed to force out of Daems.

He realised he'd wasted valuable gardening time. An hour later his labours were once again interrupted. But this time his visitor was female and welcome. He couldn't believe his luck. Josina was back.

"Well, what brings you here again? I'm afraid my uncle is out and I'm not sure when he'll be back. You're welcome to wait though – in fact you can help if you like." He looked at the highly polished leather boots she was wearing. "I can offer you a change of footwear." She nodded and he fetched a spare pair of wellington boots from the shed. "They're a bit on the large side but with this pair of thick socks you should be OK."

They worked away together and finished the row. Ryck thought the moment was opportune.

"How would you feel about going out sometime, maybe to a movie?" She stared at him and then grinned.

"So your uncle hasn't told you about our conversation the other day?" Ryck shook his head. "No, I thought not. Well I'll have to enlighten you. How do you feel about me being a relative of yours?" Ryck dropped the spade he'd been holding and it clanged onto the concrete path.

"Can you run that past me again? Are you marrying into the family or something?"

"Sorry, I should have been a bit clearer." She explained about his uncle and her mother, her face reddening as she told the story. Ryck was stunned. He stared down at the spade lying on the path and wondered how it had got there.

"So that means my uncle…I mean this must have been when Auntie Margriet was still alive…what does that make us, sort of cousins I suppose. And there's me asking you out!"

They stood looking at each other not sure what to say. Then she hugged him and told him there was nothing to stop them being friends if he could cope with that. Ryck thought it was good having an instant new relative and that the 'friends' thing could work.

They sat in the kitchen eating pancakes and drinking fruit juice. She told him about her mother and the father who'd brought her up. Ryck told her about the father who'd disappeared. When the phone rang, he was in two minds about whether to answer it or leave it to go to answerphone. He decided to let it ring. When the caller started to leave a message he recognised the voice and grabbed the handset.

"Kim hi, it's Ryck. How's it going?"

"Oh, not well I'm afraid, Ryck. Is my dad there?" Ryck explained. "No, that doesn't surprise me. He's always out. Anyway, as I told Dad, Patrick's left me and I'm really missing him." She proceeded to tell her cousin every detail of Patrick's departure and how she felt about it. The monologue went on and on without a break. Ryck held the phone away from his ear and gestured with a grin and raised eyebrows to Josina.

"Anyway, Ryck, I'm flying over tomorrow. I'll be staying with Eddie. Me and Dad will be at each other's throats within a couple of hours if I stay at his. Can you tell him to come over to Eddie's? You should come as well."

"I will, Kim. That'll be good." He told her about their grandma being in hospital, but she didn't sound all that concerned. "Oh and I've got some other important news for you. It's about your dad. But I'm not going to tell you until we meet up. In fact it'll probably be better if he tells you himself." Ryck wondered if she'd taken in his comment as she didn't respond at all. But he was used to the way she could just switch off suddenly.

"Will you want a lift from the airport?"

"No thanks. I'll get a taxi. Text me what time you and Dad will be arriving at Eddie's." With that, she was gone. Ryck told Josina about her step-sister and brother.

"Eddie will be fine about you, but Kim makes a drama about everything. She'll be OK in the end, but she'll take her time coming round to it. So don't take offence. But enough of all that. How about taking the dog for a walk?" Josina looked surprised.

"I don't remember seeing a dog when I was here last time." Ryck explained how he'd acquired Barto as a little present for his uncle.

Nineteen

Ryck was awake. He peered at his watch on the bedside table. It took him a while to decipher that it was just after 5:00am. He'd been dreaming about the bike. If only he'd kept it in the lock-up, Daems would never have found it there. Trust him to visit when the bike was in the shed. Still, he'd got the truth out of him. Well, at least – it had sounded like the truth.

He could hear activity in the room next door, his uncle's room – vigorous activity. He placed his ear close to the dividing wall and tried to separate out the various groans and sighs. Katerine must be in there with him. He was impressed with their stamina. He wondered whether Josina was also listening in from her own room. They'd lost track of time during the evening and she'd taken up Ryck's offer to stay over, rather than try and get back to her mother's house in Leuven. He'd sorted out bedding for her in the small boxroom at the end of the corridor. Before he'd gone to bed, he'd left a note on the kitchen table for his uncle, explaining there were two unexpected overnight guests in the house, but Ryck guessed from the sound of the unrestrained activity through the dividing wall that his uncle probably hadn't seen the note.

He waited a while until things went quiet and then made his way silently to the toilet, only to face the embarrassment of bumping into his uncle in the hallway. Vos was dressed in boxer shorts and a 'Visit Antwerp' t-shirt. Ryck was always impressed by the size of the scar on his uncle's right leg.

"Didn't realise you were here," Vos said in an exaggerated whisper.

"Yeah, I left a note for you. Josina's here as well." Vos looked puzzled and then, suddenly, very worried.

"Er…Ryck…look about Josina, the thing is…" His nephew interrupted him.

"Don't worry, she told me all about you and her mother. There are certain things step-cousins don't get up to."

"Keep your voice down will you?" Vos gestured towards his bedroom door. "Katerine's in there."

"Oh, I'm well aware of that, Uncle!" Ryck said as he went into the bathroom. Vos was left standing in the hallway, alone and blushing.

Over early morning coffee and potato cakes, Ryck talked to his uncle about Josina and told him he was pleased to have a new relative – if a little surprised. Vos was relieved.

"Oh, and Kim phoned. As you know, Patrick's buggered off again and she's feeling really down. She's coming to Eddie's tomorrow – no hang on, make that today and she wants you to be there." Vos groaned. He had too much on his plate already, without having to deal with Kim.

"You'll be able to tell her and Eddie about Josina, won't you?" Vos felt sheepish, nodded slowly and told Ryck that he'd rather have his teeth pulled out.

"Well here's something to cheer you up then." Ryck stuffed another potato cake into his mouth. "I imprisoned that Daems feller yesterday and got him to tell me what really happened with Moise." Vos thought he should go back to bed and try starting the day again.

"I don't think I can cope with this alone, Ryck. Can you wait until Katerine's up and you two can swap news. I'm a bit worried about her. Maybe she's not quite who I thought she was and…what on earth…?" Vos was distracted by the sight of a dog wandering into the kitchen. It went up to Ryck who patted it on the head, pulled out a bowl from under the sink, fetched a bag of dog biscuits and filled the bowl.

"You two have met before. This is Barto. He lives here now."

+ + +

Vos' stomach rumbled, but it seemed a bit early for lunch. He was trying to shake off a persistent feeling of being continually on shaky ground. He had no idea what he was going to do with the dog, was trying to steel himself to break the news about Josina to his offspring, had the small matter of his mother's future to sort out and on top of all that, Katerine was worrying him. Still it felt oddly pleasant to have the four of them, a strange sort of family, sitting around the table, drinking coffee and talking calmly to each other, the dog snoozing under the table. This new family of his seemed to have none of the stresses and strains of his old one.

Ryck asked his uncle whether he'd contacted his brother Pieter.

"I did indeed. He's really chuffed about his girlfriend. They're both coming here, so I'll be able to meet her. You might want to come along as well." Ryck said he'd look forward to it. Vos continued. "So, tell us what you managed to get out of prisoner Daems then?"

Ryck went into full flow, elaborating and embellishing his tale a little and giving a passable imitation of Daems' accent. Josina looked a little puzzled and asked Ryck to explain who Daems was and what had happened. Vos wondered whether she'd be able to handle the full details of the story.

"Well, Moise – his second name is Okator by the way. Daems told me his little secret. He hadn't even told his boss. It should help you to track his family down, Katerine. Where was I? Oh yes, Moise had been on the boat with three other illegals. Daems said that's the number they usually carried – any more than that and they'd be too conspicuous when they went ashore. When the other three had been taken off the boat under cover of darkness at Zeebrugge, Moise was unhappy. He was told he had to continue on the boat to Oostende. Apparently Rodenbach has another enterprise there of some sort. It seems that Moise panicked. He attacked Daems with a sharpened piece of metal. Daems showed me the wound, but of course he couldn't prove it was Moise's doing. Anyway Daems punched his assailant hard in the kidneys. Moise fell backwards over the low rail into the sea. He went straight under. Daems reckoned that he probably couldn't swim. He didn't resurface. Rodenbach had been below deck and hadn't seen any of this. When Daems finally plucked up the courage to tell him, they'd lost valuable time. They spent a good while looking for Moise, before deciding to head back to Zeebrugge. Rodenbach was in a foul mood and kept talking about the money he'd lose and how it would be bad for business.

Once they'd docked Rodenbach had taken the Jeep out and searched De Haan beach where he'd calculated the body would wash up. It's a really long stretch of beach, so Rodenbach was lucky to find the body, but as Daems said, his boss grew up with the beaches, tides and currents and knows the area like the back of his hand. Of course when it came to it, you and Simone just beat him to the discovery of the body," Ryck said looking at his uncle. "And we know what happened after that."

"So, what actually killed him then?" Josina asked.

"Daems thought he drowned, claimed he didn't hit him hard enough for it to have been a fatal blow. But who knows." Ryck paused and took a sip of water.

"What a sad story," Josina said. "What happened to Moise's body after he'd been found on the beach?"

"Daems told me they buried him at sea. Of course I've only got his word for that, but I suppose it would make sense – I mean, from their point of view."

"Of course this will never become a court case," Vos said drily. "The only person who saw Rodenbach, the vehicle and Moise's body was Simone Josse and unfortunately, she's no longer with us."

Katerine, who thought that Josina might be feeling overwhelmed by all this, put her arm round her shoulder.

"You don't have to listen, love. You can always sit in the other room." Josina sniffed, blew her nose and said she'd stay. Vos announced that they needed food. The fridge was almost empty, so he phoned for pizzas, warmed some plates and fetched some bottles of beer from the shed. They sat drinking beer and picking at a bowl of peanuts, waiting for the pizzas to arrive.

"I think it's time for your story, Katerine. I know you've been putting it off, but maybe you should take the floor." Ryck couldn't quite gauge his uncle's tone of voice which sounded almost critical. He wondered what had happened in Brussels. He assumed that it couldn't be anything too serious, given the sounds that had come from their bedroom earlier that morning. Vos' phone rang just as Katerine was starting to speak.

"Who? Oh, it's you, Mr Wouters. Actually I'm busy just now. I'll call you back." Vos raised his eyes to the ceiling. "What do you mean your house? I'm afraid that's not possible. My mother will come here when she's well enough to leave the hospital. Hold on, hold on. You can't be leaving now. Please put my mother on the line now!" Vos waited, looking increasingly agitated. The doorbell rang and Ryck went to answer it. "Mother, what's this nonsense Wouters is talking about? … But you're coming here, I told you. I'm not always out and anyway it wouldn't be proper for you to be living in another man's house." The words were out before Vos had had time to think about them. "Mother! Mother?"

He slammed the phone down on the kitchen table. Ryck put the pizza boxes, the warmed plates and a pile of forks on the table and they all helped themselves.

"So, Uncle, Grandma's going to Wouter's house then? She'll be fine there, you know – I've been there, it's a bungalow, no steps, shower room, it'll be perfect for her. And Mr Wouters is OK. He's on the level and it's obvious he cares a lot for Grandma." Ryck pulled at a slice of pizza, jerking it to snap the strands of cheese that clung to it obstinately. Vos stared at his nephew.

"How do you know all this?" Before Ryck had chance to explain, Vos continued. "I'll have to go round there as soon as I've finished this pizza. I'm afraid your story will just have to wait, Katerine." Vos turned to face Josina. "I can give you a lift to Leuven, once I've called in to see my mother. Would that be OK?" She nodded and thanked him.

When the two of them left, Ryck slid seamlessly into the role of host and topped up the beer glasses.

"So, Katerine – now's your chance to tell me exactly what happened in Brussels."

+ + +

Vos knew he was in the wrong – there was no need for his gruff and aggressive manner. In contrast, Wouters was calm and welcoming, showed him round his bungalow and made it clear that he wanted to help.

"But of course it's up to your mother to decide where she wants to live. I'll leave you two to talk it over. I'll be in the conservatory if you need me."

Mrs Vos sat in an armchair with a plaid blanket over her knees. With obvious pleasure, she used the control panel to adjust the footrest. Her coffee mug was firmly anchored in a well in the arm of the chair. She nibbled carefully at a chocolate biscuit, making sure she caught the few stray crumbs on her floral-patterned plate.

"Thank you for coming, Harry. I know this can't be easy for you. Mr Wouters – Jan – is a very kind man. I've known him for

a year or two – not that you'd be aware of that. It's one area where
your detection skills have let you down. We're good for each other.
And let's face it, you and I have always rubbed each other up the
wrong way, whenever we've been together for too long, so living
with you wouldn't really be a good thing, for either of us. You'd have
to stay home when you wanted to be out. Just look at this recent
investigation of yours. I won't pretend I understand why you do it,
but it's clear to me that you enjoy it so I wouldn't want to be holding
you back. You're not an old man yet and, who knows, you may find
yourself another partner one day. In fact from what you told me the
other day – you may have done that already. I wouldn't want to be
the gooseberry." Vos couldn't remember his mother being so open
with her feelings before. Everything she said was true.

He took her hand and told her that if she was happy doing this
then that was all that mattered, but that there'd always be space for
her in his home. He could see her eyes moistening but she didn't
cry. He was hesitant, but felt this was as good an opportunity as any.

"Would you feel up to having a visitor, Mother, just for a few
minutes?"

"What, here, now?" He nodded. "Well I suppose so, but it's up
to Mr Wouters. After all it's his house. Who is it?"

"Remember I told you about my new daughter." It sounded
odd to Vos to use these words, but he couldn't think of a better
way of putting it. "Josina, she's in the car – I'm giving her a lift to
Leuven. I'd like you to meet her, just for a minute or two."

"Well I don't suppose it can do any harm. You seem pretty
sure she is your daughter even though you've got no proof." Vos
ignored her comment and said he'd ask Mr Wouters if it was OK.

When Josina walked into the sitting room a few minutes later,
Mrs Vos took a sharp intake of breath.

"You could be Kim's sister, my dear!"

+ + +

"So when did you realise that Hendrickx was First Base?" Ryck asked.

"From the information on Simone's C.D," Katerine said. "I put two and two together and luckily I was right."

Ryck looked impressed.

"So, can I get this straight, Kat? What you're saying is that the Group operate a people-smuggling business, but it's one with a conscience? I must say, until you mentioned it, I didn't realise it was so difficult for Congolese migrants to get here legitimately. Isn't there a risk though that this sort of thing could get out of hand? I mean the conscience bit might go out of the window if you got someone in charge with an eye for the profits to be made?"

Katerine realised she shouldn't underestimate Harry's nephew.

"Spot on, Ryck. I've been asking myself the same question ever since I came face to face with Hendrickx. Look, you need to keep what I'm telling you under your hat. There's something about Hendrickx that doesn't ring true, but I can't put my finger on it. As I said, I've been dealing with the Group for years on the cultural side. It fits in well with what I do at the university and they're great when it comes to contacting the right people in the DRC, fixing me up with places to stay out in the sticks and alerting me to the constantly changing dangers. They can open doors which otherwise I'd be stuck the wrong side of."

"So you spend quite a bit of time over there?"

"I always have done – not just in the DRC but in other parts of West Africa as well. Of course the university doesn't know about the people-smuggling. I'd be out on my ear if they did. We have to be careful to keep all that activity under the radar. But I have to be honest with you and Harry. I've known about the people-smuggling all along. In fact I've been involved at the DRC end. Some of the people I come in contact with lead such terrible lives and through First Base – that's Hendrickx as you know – they're put into contact with the guys who organise the journeys north. Obviously what we do is illegal, but the Group makes some money out of it which can be ploughed into their legit work and the migrants get to live and work here. There aren't any real losers."

"That's difficult for me to get my head round," Ryck said. "What with all the stuff in the papers about illegal immigration and the way the Government goes on about it?"

"Yes, I know Ryck. That's what I used to think. Maybe I'm too close to it now. If there were more visas available, it wouldn't be necessary." Ryck didn't look convinced. "By the way, I haven't had chance to thank you for finding out Moise's surname. That's the final piece of the jigsaw and we should be able to find his family now. When we do, Harry and I will take the compensation money out to them." Ryck looked surprised.

"What – you'll both be going to the DRC?" Katerine nodded. "That's really good," Ryck continued, "except isn't there a danger the money might end up in the wrong hands, you know, hangers on? I mean – 10k, it's a lot of cash. And how will you actually take it into the country? It must be above their cash import limit surely."

"I've got this suitcase, with a false bottom. It sounds corny, I know, but it works – I've done it before. Anyway they're more interested in guns and drugs than money. And if the worst comes to the worst, we'd just have to pay them off. We might lose the lot, but I think that would be unlikely." Ryck topped up the beer glasses.

"I'm really hoping Harry will wind his case up now and be finished with the lot of them – Rodenbach, Daems and Hendrickx," Katerine said, draining her glass.

Twenty

Hendrickx didn't much like travelling out of Brussels, but enjoyed driving the Audi. It had always been a dream of his when he'd been a boy, flicking through his uncle's car magazines, to own a big, powerful, comfortable car. He switched on cruise control, turned off the musical wallpaper on the radio and took another small chocolate from the tray on the passenger seat. He was a man who liked his work and couldn't imagine what he'd do without it. He had no hobbies or real interests, apart from the men in his life, and no family to speak of, but felt he was unusually lucky. He was making money – lots of it – and doing good at the same time. Not that others saw his efforts in quite the same light, but who cared? The only downside to his life and it was a big one, was his addiction to the upmarket casinos he frequented. There was something about the atmosphere of these places he couldn't resist – smooth, orderly, well run. Large sums of money were won and lost, but it all happened with a certain level of decorum. Hendrickx knew he should stop. His debts weren't completely unmanageable but things were getting tight.

He pulled into a lay-by, made a brief phone call and took a few minutes to think about Katerine. He'd built up a very clear image of Bookworm over years of emailing and still hadn't got over his surprise that his correspondent was a woman. They worked well as a team. Through her university work, Bookworm had the links on the ground in the DRC and other parts of West Africa and he, as First Base, was the main contact with the smugglers and had the business links in Belgium. Between them they provided a comprehensive service.

As he started up the Audi, Hendrickx wondered yet again whether it had been really necessary to hand over the five thousand. He'd done it for peace of mind, but it was a lot of money.

He'd only been to Rodenbach's place at Zeebrugge once before but he remembered the route clearly. He'd always had the ability to remember directions without having to write anything down. Even as a child he'd had this in-built radar.

Although Rodenbach was expecting him, he didn't look at all pleased when Hendrickx arrived and asked bluntly what his rare visit was all about.

"You should know the answer to that. Fatalities tend to bring unwelcome attention and I don't mean just the police. The man who's been dogging your footsteps is unpredictable and that could be very dangerous for us. By the way – what's his name?" Rodenbach told him. "Well, you're lucky, very lucky. I've bought Vos off, so he shouldn't trouble us anymore."

"What do you mean – you bought him off? I'd already done that!" Rodenbach scowled at Hendrickx.

"Yes I'm well aware of that but it obviously wasn't enough. Anyway, you owe me and it's payback time."

"What the fuck do you mean by that?" Rodenbach shouted. "Look we're in this together. Your outfit needs me as much as I need you. Don't forget the final leg of the journey is the riskiest bit – it's my neck on the line. We had a problem locally, we sorted it. Vos may be too nosy for his own good but he can't prove anything. And the woman's dead – but that was down to providence, not to me. So we carry on, unless there's something else you need to get off your chest, Mr Hendrickx."

"As a matter of fact, there is."

+ + +

Eddie didn't really get on with his sister. It had been a different story when they were younger, but they'd grown apart. He thought she'd become selfish and out of touch with the family. She thought he was a stick in the mud. They rarely saw each other. Having to put Kim up for a couple of nights was a big concession for Eddie, but he didn't want to disappoint his dad.

Kim arrived by taxi in the middle of a squally shower. She used her charms to persuade the taxi driver to walk with her to Eddie's front door and provide protection for her expensive coat in the form of a large umbrella. He used his other hand to wheel her heavy suitcase along. Kim was encumbered only by a small, fashionably understated handbag, which she clutched under one arm. She dismissed the driver and greeted Eddie. It was a good start he thought. She seemed calm and composed. He showed her to her room and left her for the good half hour he knew it would take her to wash, change and 'adjust' as she always put it.

Eddie was relieved that his wife, Sibilla, was still at work. He was nervous about what his father wanted to talk about. Over the phone, he'd just said it was something important to do with the family.

Eddie had spoken to Ryck who said he'd been sworn to secrecy. But he had let the Katerine cat out of the bag and Eddie had grilled him for more detail. He hoped it would work out for his father. He was concerned about how his dad would cope if he had to continue living on his own as he got older.

Kim emerged from the bedroom, hair freshly washed and dried, wearing a very expensive-looking lilac trouser suit. She inspected the sofa to assess whether it was suitably clean and free from potentially harmful debris and then perched on the edge, one long leg crossed elegantly over the other.

"Sorry to hear about Patrick, Sis. Any sign of him coming back?" She must have expected the question and yet she looked surprised.

"No, I'm afraid this might be it." It was Eddie's turn to look surprised. This was an unusually calm response from Kim, no hysterics, no arm waving. "I think that particular chapter of my life is over." She reached in her handbag for her phone and flicked through the screens. "Here, take a look. This is Anders." She handed the phone to her brother and edged a little further back on the settee.

"He's a very nice looking young man. What does he do?"

"He's not that young, Eddie!" Obviously a sensitive point, he thought. "He works with me at the bank."

You'll be doubly loaded then. Eddie just managed to stop himself coming out with the comment. The flat was unusually quiet. His sister didn't like children and he'd arranged for his two to stay with Sibilla's parents. He couldn't get used to being able to hear the tick of the clock on the mantelpiece.

As Eddie was making the coffee, his father arrived. Kim let him in and hugged him in a distant manner. He looked awkward and spoke too quickly, trying to avoid any difficult silences. Whilst they were standing in the hallway, he asked her about Patrick and she told him about Anders. Vos was relieved that no lengthy inquest would be required. Once the three of them were seated in the living room he cleared his throat. Eddie half-expected him to pull a pre-prepared speech out of his pocket.

"This is not the easiest thing to have to tell you. In fact it's one of the most difficult things I've ever had to do."

Kim interrupted him.

"You're not ill, are you, Dad?" He shook his head.

"No, dear, nothing like that. I don't want anything I say to make you think that I didn't love your mother very much. I can't emphasise that enough. But..." He faltered, took a sip of coffee and then continued. "I was unfaithful to her. Just once but, I let her down." He pulled a tissue out of his pocket and blew his nose. "The other day I had a visitor who gave me the shock of my life."

Eddie and Kim exchanged looks but remained silent. "Her name's Josina and she told me that she's my daughter."

Kim lost her grip on her coffee cup and the tepid brown liquid sprayed over her delicate lilac trousers. She cursed and ran out of the room, slamming the door as she went. Eddie shook his head.

"So, who's her mother?" It was the first thing that came into his mind. He didn't want it to be anyone he knew.

"She's called Klaar, lives in Leuven. I was away for a conference, we saw each other for one night. I'm really sorry, Eddie, really sorry." Vos sat with his head in his hands.

"These things happen, Dad, don't beat yourself up about it too much. Did Mum know?"

Vos told his son about the conversation he'd had with Margriet in the hospital shortly before she'd died. Eddie could hardly bear to think of his mother on her deathbed able to be so forgiving. The two of them sat in silence for a long while. Neither felt there was anything more to say. Finally Vos rose from his seat and told Eddie he'd have to go through and speak to Kim. He knocked on her bedroom door and waited.

"Go away, Dad. I can't speak to you about this, not now, maybe never. I've called a taxi. I'll have to stay in a hotel to escape your words which are still hanging in the air waiting for me." Vos' first instinct was to ask her what on earth she meant, but he suppressed it. It wasn't the time for that.

"OK love – if that's what you feel you have to do. But I'm really sorry and I hope you will be able to talk to me about it at some stage."

He retreated to the sitting room. Eddie poured them both a drink and they sat together in the gathering gloom. Eddie put his arm around his father's shoulder.

"You know the important thing was Mum's forgiveness. If she could do that – I'm sure we can, but it'll take Kim a while. Just leave her to it."

The taxi driver arrived and Kim walked out of her brother's flat without a backward glance.

+ + +

On his way home to Heist, Vos pulled in at a service station, filled up and bought a coffee and a bar of chocolate at the cafe. He sat on a high stool by the window and watched the unceasing line of headlights passing by. He gradually realised that a man on an adjacent stool had asked him a question and he had to turn and ask him to repeat it. But it wasn't a question. The man was in full flow about some problem with his wife. Vos couldn't cope with it. He drained his coffee and muttered something to the man about being in a hurry. He struggled to get off his stool, but finally managed to escape to his car.

Normally he loved being in Antwerp, but on this occasion he hadn't been able to get away quickly enough. Things couldn't have gone much worse with Kim and he didn't know whether she'd ever come round. At least she seemed to have got over Patrick quickly enough, but he knew that this state of affairs would last only as long as Anders, her new man, lasted.

He felt he didn't have enough space in his head for all the thinking he needed to do. Why did everything seem to happen at the same time? At the factory, his days had been planned and predictable. Of course there were problems, but they were technical and could usually be sorted out with the application of some detailed knowhow and a bit of logic. All this personal stuff was far more difficult. He missed not being able to talk to Margriet, certainly couldn't talk to his mother and speaking to Kim about almost anything was out of the question. And his friends were as bad at this sort of stuff as he was.

Once he was back on the road, he gradually began to feel better, finishing his coffee, one hand on the steering wheel. He watched the windscreen wipers struggling to cope with the heavy rain. As he hit a downhill stretch of road, he felt as if he was falling slowly down a long, wet, orange tunnel. The sensation wasn't unpleasant. It was if the car was driving itself and he was just a passenger. He was so tuned out that he almost missed the warning signs on the gantry above and the sudden flare of red lights just ahead of him. He managed to come to a halt centimetres from the bumper of the car in front. His hands were sweating and slippery on the steering wheel.

As he waited in line, his mind floated off again. Katerine was telling him about Hendrickx and about her active involvement in the people-smuggling, the way she saw it as the lesser of two evils. He realised his view was traditional – it was illegal – end of story!

The queue of traffic still stubbornly refused to move and he turned the engine off.

His biggest worry had been that she'd been using him and that she'd known all about Rodenbach's activities from the start. But she'd convinced him that she only dealt with what she called the 'upstream' work, identifying potential migrants in the DRC. The way the Group worked was that activists only knew about their own bit of the operation. She'd been told nothing about the 'downstream' activity, the actual smuggling of the migrants into the country. Likewise Rodenbach and his fellow smugglers knew nothing about her.

The traffic began to move forward slowly.

What really worried him was that their widely differing views might drive a wedge between them, but, he was relieved that so far, it didn't seem to have affected their feelings for each other. And now she wanted to take him to the DRC – and he'd never travelled anywhere out of Europe before.

By the time he reached his house, he could barely remember the final part of the journey. It seemed as if one minute he'd been waiting in the traffic jam and the next he was pulling onto his driveway.

He felt cold and tired and needed another coffee. As it brewed, he heard the doorbell and cursed. He didn't want to see anyone, let alone speak to them. All he wanted to do was sit with his coffee, put his feet up and watch the TV. He didn't care what was on – anything would do. But, whoever was at the front door wasn't giving up. He walked slowly and stiffly along the hallway, opened the door and peered out. He felt he was dreaming, rooted to the spot, one of those nightmares when it's impossible to move. The man on the doorstep was the man from the boat.

Rodenbach stood there, a bottle of brandy in his right hand. Vos could tell it was a very expensive bottle. He finally managed to speak.

"Have you come to pay me some more compensation then?"

"No, I'm here to make you a proposition. Can I come in?"

Vos wondered what on earth the man was up to. Had he come to get his revenge, to inveigle himself inside the house, before striking the killer blow? Vos thought it was unlikely. There was something about the man's demeanour, something underneath that suggested an element of contrition, maybe even vulnerability. Once he'd recovered from his initial shock, Vos found himself intrigued.

"You'd better come in I suppose." Vos led Rodenbach to the kitchen and fetched two crystal glasses. His visitor broke the seal on the bottle and poured out two large measures. "Let's hear your proposition then." Vos tried to adopt a neutral tone, neither friendly nor hostile.

Rodenbach sipped his drink slowly and looked round the kitchen, at the ornaments on the mantelpiece and the family photographs on the dresser.

"So this is where you hit Daems, is it? He told me all about it." Vos was annoyed and was about to interrupt, but Rodenbach carried on. "No doubt you have your own version of events and I'd be more inclined to believe yours than his. Not that he's with me anymore. Anyway – enough of that! The reason I'm here, well it's all down to Sabina really, you know, the woman I live with. You met her." Vos nodded. "She told me I had to sort this problem out or she'd leave me and it was no idle threat. I know what she's like. She told me to hire you so that's why I've come, Mr Vos."

"What on earth do you mean – hire me?"

Rodenbach scanned the room again as if he was looking for something particular.

"It's quite simple really – I hear you're a private eye of some sort and I want to pay you to do a job."

Vos thought his tiredness was affecting his hearing or his judgement or both. Rodenbach topped up the glasses and continued. "My problem is with Mr Hendrickx. Let me tell you about him."

"I already know about him," Vos said sharply. "I know about him and I know about his group." Rodenbach didn't look surprised. Vos replaced his glass on the coaster which depicted a view of the Brussels Atomium. "I haven't actually met him but I know enough about him and his activities. The trouble is," Vos continued, "it's one of those moral dilemmas. If I were to succeed in getting his people-smuggling business closed down, would that be to the overall benefit of our small section of mankind or to its detriment?"

"I think what I'm about to tell you now will help you to decide what to do," Rodenbach said. "Hendrickx just paid me a visit. He's only ever done that once before. He came to tell me what I'd be doing next – tell me, not ask me. He's moving into trafficking – forcing women into the sex trade to be precise. When I told him I wouldn't get involved he said I didn't have a choice. Since I'd compromised his operations by losing a man overboard, I'd lost my freedom to choose."

Vos wasn't exactly sure what the difference was between smuggling and trafficking, apart from the money. He thought it must be to do with how migrants were used – or rather abused – once they'd reached their destination. He tried not to think about whether Katerine knew about Hendrickx's plans.

"So where do I come into all this?" Vos couldn't see what possible role he could have in this argument between a crook and a bigger crook.

"I want you to gather evidence for me – it's what you do, isn't it?" Vos thought he saw a slight flicker of a smile on the other man's face. "I'll explain."

Twenty-One

Ryck thought he'd done a good job in persuading Katerine to tell him what had really happened in Brussels. He'd felt relieved, in a way, when she'd said she hoped Harry would be giving up his investigations, but part of him was disappointed that the excitement was over. He'd enjoyed his alternative life.

He measured the first length of wallpaper, making neat pencil marks before carefully cutting the floral patterned paper to shape. It was possibly the last pattern he'd ever have chosen himself, but his customers were usually very clear about what they wanted. He'd watch them leafing through the pages of his sample books, shaking their heads repeatedly until they alighted on the design they'd been waiting for.

He placed the paper on the table and applied the paste smoothly and evenly. There was something pleasantly hypnotic about the whole process and he liked to watch the new wall slowly creeping its way around the room. When he reached the half-way mark, he stopped and poured himself a drink from his flask. He sat on the back doorstep and looked out across the flat open fields beyond.

In the end he hadn't gone with his uncle to Antwerp to see Eddie and Kim. Normally he'd have jumped at the chance to see Kim on one of her rare visits back home, but he'd had a distinct feeling that this particular visit would not go well. And from what Eddie had told him since, he'd been right.

By four in the afternoon, he'd finished the room and he stood back to admire his handiwork. He packed up his equipment, folded the table, placed the unused roll of paper in a protective tube and stored it all temporarily in the shed in the back garden. He'd come to this arrangement with the house owner, a man in his eighties, who'd told Ryck he'd been born in the house and had never lived anywhere else. Ryck had realised with some embarrassment that he was a one-house man himself.

He opened his rucksack, put his flask and sandwich box back in and pulled out his laptop. He'd been meaning to check out the other CDs in Simone Josse's collection. He'd had a nagging feeling that Simone might have unearthed more information about Hendrickx.

He methodically pushed each of the CDs in turn into his laptop. With the third one, which was labeled as a Beethoven symphony, he struck lucky. Far from being German classical music, the CD actually contained another of Simone's research reports. Judging by the date of the report Ryck thought it had probably been her last piece of work. She'd unearthed evidence of a plan by Hendrickx to branch out into people-trafficking. According to her notes, nobody else in the Group was aware of this. It was very much Hendrickx's own private enterprise.

Ryck knew he had to speak to Katerine. He rang her mobile. It was difficult for him to make himself heard over the noise of her commuter train. When she finally realised what he was telling her, she told him she had a confession to make.

"Look Ryck, I already know about this. Harry told me, but he swore me to secrecy. He found out from Rodenbach and now he's going after Hendrickx." Ryck wondered if he'd heard her correctly – Rodenbach? She explained what had happened as best she could. "It sounds really dangerous to me and I'm worried. He's driving to Jalloh's apartment in Brussels."

Ryck went home and pushed a change of clothes into his

rucksack. He took the back roads to Mechelen, parked the Vespa at the station, bought a ticket and boarded the Brussels train.

+ + +

When Vos had phoned Katerine to tell her about his 'commission' from Rodenbach they'd had a proper row. She said he'd be crazy to get involved while he told her she was compromised because of her longstanding links with Hendrickx. The phone call had ended abruptly.

Vos was back in Jalloh's apartment, which was beginning to feel like a second home. Like Katerine, Jalloh was extremely wary about Vos' idea of working with Rodenbach, but he soon realised that he wouldn't be able to persuade him to change his mind.

"Where are you going to be then – on the boat or on the shore? You'll have to make a choice." Jalloh's voice was firm.

"I don't like idea of the boat, particularly if it's rough out there. I'll have to cover things from the shore. I was hoping you might be able to take the boat.

"I can't help you out Harry," Jalloh said, "because Hendrickx knows me. If he spotted me, he'd know something was up. We're not exactly friends. What I don't understand is how come you trust Rodenbach all of a sudden? He was the big enemy last time we met and now you're cosying up to him."

"Something about him has changed J. He seems to have drawn a line which he won't cross. For me, maybe it's a case of my enemy's enemy is my friend! Rodenbach and I have now got a mutual interest in nailing Hendrickx."

Later, as he lay in bed unable to sleep, Vos felt his confidence waning. What was he doing? What had started as a simple desire to find out how a man had died was now turning into a crusade. Perhaps Katerine was right. Damn it, of course she was right, but he knew he wouldn't back down. And he still had to find someone to cover the boat.

He heard the front door opening below him, scraping on the uneven hall floor. Vos realised Jalloh was still up. The door slammed shut. There were voices. He tried to pick up on the conversation, but Jalloh and his visitor were speaking too softly.

He continued to hear voices which got gradually louder. He was sure he could hear the De Backer factory supervisor talking. What was he doing here? And then another voice, not Jalloh's, but a voice he didn't recognise. Suddenly there were two men in his room. What were they saying? They wanted to know why he was letting the machines stand idle, why he'd turned off the power. He turned over and the men disappeared.

+ + +

Vos woke early and tried to disentangle his dreams from the reality of the morning. He tiptoed downstairs to make himself a drink. As he walked through the living room to the kitchen he was startled to see someone sleeping on Jalloh's sofa, curled up under a thick blanket. He filled the kettle, turned it on and searched through the cupboards for coffee. When Ryck's voice floated in from the sitting room telling him not to be so noisy, Vos was convinced he must still be dreaming. He peered cautiously around the sitting room door and realised that he was fully awake.

"Morning Uncle!" Ryck pushed the blanket off and struggled to sit up. "This is my little surprise. The team is back in harness."

"I don't have a clue what you're talking about, Ryck." Vos was exasperated.

"It's simple. I'll be covering the boat while you cover the shore. Jalloh told me all about it." They heard footsteps on the stairs and Jalloh came into the sitting room saying he was pleased to see they'd 'introduced' themselves and asking if they wanted eggs for breakfast. They both nodded and thanked him.

Vos scratched his head and asked his nephew how he knew what was going on.

"Look," Ryck continued. "I phoned Katerine yesterday to tell her I'd found some new information about Henrickx, about him branching out into people trafficking. It was on one of Simone's CDs. Anyway Katerine told me that you already knew about this and that you'd re-opened the case – something to do with Rodenbach of all people. She didn't ask me to do anything. It was my decision to come here and it looks like it's a good job I did. You can't cover the boat and the shore can you?"

Vos wondered what his sister would have to say if she knew about her son's continued involvement in this increasingly risky investigation. But when he looked closely at Ryck, as if for the first time in years, he saw him as he really was – a man of almost thirty – rather than his little nephew. He realised Ryck was old enough to make his own decisions.

"If you're sure you want to help, that's fine by me. In fact I'd be really grateful. We can sort our plans out on the drive to Zeebrugge. Rodenbach has left a car there for me to use, so you'll need to drive my car back to Brussels, once you've finished on the boat." Ryck nodded.

He spent the whole of breakfast talking non-stop with Jalloh. Vos couldn't understand how he was able to do this. On the surface the two men had little if anything in common and yet the conversation flowed, as if they were old friends. As they were leaving, Jalloh gave them a bag of sandwiches, a flask of coffee… and a final warning about the dangers that lay ahead.

+ + +

Ryck was disappointed that there wasn't more of a swell as the *Leopold* chugged away from the shelter of Zeebrugge harbour, out into the open sea. He watched the dockside ships slowly receding and listened to the rapid conversations of the five black women who were seated in a ring, smoking and drinking. It was officially one of the *Leopold* hen party nights, a calm evening, a hint of warmth still in the air, coloured lights strung along the sides of the boat and a huge speaker pumping out bass-heavy music. Ryck didn't recognise it – something West African he thought. He could see Rodenbach's woman in the wheelhouse and he tried to control his fantasies, knowing it wasn't a good time to lose concentration. The skipper himself was below deck. He'd said a few words to Ryck as they'd boarded, to make sure he'd been properly briefed, but had then reverted to his usual taciturn manner.

Ryck was in two minds about what he was doing. Part of him regretted his impetuous – his mother would have said reckless – decision to go on this particular trip. He asked himself what was the worst that could happen and a voice, deep and loud, answered that of course he could die – after all the *Leopold* had already set a precedent for losing a man overboard. But another voice told him to forget about the risks and think instead about the excitement, how it was preferable to hanging yet another length of wallpaper.

Someone tapped him on the shoulder and he turned to find it was one of the women. She asked him if he'd like to dance. Instinctively he looked for Rodenbach. After all he had a job to do, but he had no idea whether it included dancing with passengers. There was no sign of the man. He looked into the woman's eyes and looked away again immediately. He wasn't sure he could handle the promise that lay there. She led him into the middle of the deck and they showed off their respective moves. He preferred the slower numbers where she held him close and breathed softly into his ear. She told him she'd won the bet for who got to dance with him. The other women looked on and clapped at the end of each number.

Rodenbach made a brief appearance above deck, glanced at the proceedings and disappeared again. Beyond the boat, it was completely dark, apart from the lights of the occasional ship on the horizon. After about an hour Rodenbach reappeared on deck and spoke briefly to one of the women. The sound system was switched off. Ryck's dancing partner kissed him on the lips and rejoined her friends. He stood in a daze by the rail at the front of the boat. As he gradually recovered his senses, he peered into the darkness ahead, checked that the night-vision camera was attached to his belt and waited.

The coaster loomed on their port side. Ryck, partially hidden behind the wheelhouse silently recorded the scene as it unfolded – the dark shapes leaning on the coaster's rail, the five passengers making their way hesitantly down a temporary stairway – clearly reluctant to step into the bobbing dinghy – its slow progress across the watery gap between the two bigger boats and then the new passengers' final climb onto the safety of the deck of the *Leopold*. Ryck heard a shout from the coaster and Rodenbach's growled reply. Though he couldn't hear what was said, he managed to get a clear shot of the man on the other vessel, who, almost comically, was wearing a captain's hat.

The hen party made the reverse journey, laughing and joking as they floated away towards the coaster. Once the exchange was completed, there was a final exchange of shouts between the two boats and then the coaster pulled away.

The newly-arrived women had a cowed, defeated look and sat huddled together close to the wheelhouse. Rodenbach prowled the deck nervously as the *Leopold* started the homeward leg of the journey, scanning the horizon and glancing at his watch intermittently. He went to the wheelhouse and spoke to Sabina and then returned to take up his lookout position. He must have spotted something. He returned to the wheelhouse, the coloured lights came back on and the sound system burst in to life. He ordered the women to stand and dance. Their reluctance was obvious, until Sabina spoke to each of them in turn.

A cutter approached to starboard, its searchlight dazzling. An order was issued by megaphone and the *Leopold*'s engine fell silent. As the vessel stopped moving, two men in customs uniforms boarded. Rodenbach was there instantly with a clipboard holding a sheaf of papers. Out of earshot of the customs men, Sabina spoke to the women again in a calm, low voice. Ryck tried to look inconspicuous.

+ + +

Vos was feeling the cold as he sat in the anonymous looking Ford that Rodenbach had provided. He zipped up his fleece, pulled his hat down lower over his ears and reached for Jalloh's flask. There were still plenty of vehicles in the dockside car park. Vos had been worried that the cars might thin out too much and leave the Ford somewhat exposed. He wondered where all the drivers were. They surely couldn't all be out on the high seas. It was just approaching ten – not much longer to wait if Rodenbach had got his timings right.

Vos was parked in a dimly lit corner away from the spread of light beaming down from the high metal columns. He could see the car park entrance and kept a close eye on the comings and goings. It reminded him of a surveillance he'd done on a summer's evening, a few years ago, when he'd been trying to track down an errant husband. He'd fallen asleep in the warmth of the car and woken in the middle of the night only to find that all the other cars had disappeared and he'd been locked in the car park.

He resisted the temptation to turn on the heater. He had the radio on a 'low light' as his father used to say, a commentary on a match between Standard Liege and Club Bruges. The game was a defensive stalemate and it didn't help Vos with his attempts to stay awake. He retuned to Klara, but the harpsichord recital was about as stimulating as the football match. He turned the radio off and thought about his women – his mother, his daughter and his – what was she? His lover, his girlfriend? He reached for his phone to text her and then changed his mind. He didn't need the distraction.

No sooner had he put the phone back in his pocket, when a grey, Renault people-carrier drove into the car park and flashed its lights twice. A black Mercedes van returned the signal and five women were ushered from the Renault into the van. The doors closed rapidly and the Renault turned right out of the car park and sped off. The Mercedes turned left at a more sedate speed. Vos lowered his camera and started the engine. With night-vision, it had been a simple task to capture the transfer and it made him feel almost like a professional. He followed the Mercedes at a safe distance.

Once it joined the E40 the vehicle ahead increased its speed, but kept within the limit. Vos relaxed, guessing it would be a while before they'd turn off the motorway. Traffic was light. When he turned the radio on again, the harpsichord music had thankfully come to an end and the Sibelius symphony that followed was much more to his liking. He'd always wanted to go to Finland – all those lakes and forests. He glanced in the rear view mirror out of habit and then looked again. He couldn't be certain but the vehicle behind looked suspiciously like the Renault from the car park. He'd no way of knowing whether they were just riding shotgun or whether they'd spotted him. He told himself it was his punishment for allowing himself to relax.

They hit the spaghetti junction of the R0 on the outskirts of Brussels and Vos followed the Mercedes as it turned off onto the N9. Rodenbach hadn't known where the ultimate destination of the new migrants would be – just that it would be somewhere in Brussels. Vos had to concentrate hard as he followed the van, which was a couple of vehicles up ahead. As they approached the Weststation, the Mercedes turned off onto a small industrial estate. Vos had to make a quick decision. He could either carry straight on and see whether the Renault was following him and risk losing the Mercedes, or turn on to the estate and risk being trapped between the two vehicles. He decided he had to follow the Mercedes. He held his breath as he turned, his eyes glued to the rear view mirror. The Renault continued along the N9 towards Anderlecht. Vos remembered to breathe out, switched his vision to the windscreen and just caught sight of the Mercedes turning into the car park of a small industrial unit. He switched his lights off and cruised to a halt.

Once out of the vehicle, he edged forward to a brick wall which surrounded the car park. It was high enough to give him some cover, but low enough for him to be able to take a series of shots of the women being ushered out of the van by two men who'd emerged from the modern warehouse building. They were led away into the warehouse.

Vos ducked down below the wall and texted Jalloh to let him know the location of the traffickers' drop-off point. Just as he was about to return to his car, he noticed one of the traffickers making his way from the car park towards the Ford. Vos hadn't locked the vehicle because he'd wanted to avoid the inevitable bleeping sounds which would have followed. The keys were in his fleece pocket. He tried to remember what incriminating evidence he might have left in the car. He patted the zipped pockets of his trousers to check that wallet, notebook, phone and camera were all there. The trafficker tried the door of the Ford, opened it, leaned in and rummaged around. He emerged with a flask in one hand and a newspaper in the other and ran back to the car park, calling out in a low voice.

+ + +

Ryck had waited for an hour, as instructed, before setting off in Vos' car back to Brussels. He'd been impressed with the way

Rodenbach had handled the customs officers when they'd boarded the boat. He'd previously viewed the skipper as just a hothead, but the man had stayed calm, told the officers it was just another of his hen party trips and showed them the paper work with the names of the passengers and crew – all Belgian passport-holders. The customs men had seemed only mildly interested, a routine check providing a short interlude in an otherwise dull and boring night shift on coastal patrol.

Ryck reached Jalloh's flat and used a spare key to let himself in. He checked his phone. There was a message from Jalloh. His man had picked up the target and would text details of the morning rendezvous as soon as he knew them. Ryck was far too wound up to contemplate sleep. He turned on the TV and half-watched an episode of Columbo. He followed the gist of what was being said as he ate from a large bowl of fresh fruit and wondered what was delaying his uncle's return.

+ + +

Vos watched the three men as they examined the Ford. He could just about pick up their conversation. They were undecided about what to do. Eventually two of them returned to the industrial unit and the third waited in the car, slumped down low in the driver's seat.

Vos knew he had to cut his losses. There was a hilly landscaped area behind him. He edged along the car park wall, glancing occasionally at the Ford. He tried to keep low as he moved slowly up the hill towards the trees at the summit, but his right knee was awkwardly unresponsive. He heard the door of the Ford open and saw the man jump out and start running towards him. Vos tried to quicken his pace. He reached the cover of the trees, ran over the crest of the hill and started down the far side, the sound of his pursuer's shouts getting ever nearer. At the bottom of the hill was a large ornamental lake. To his left he could see a high fence. He ran right along the shore of the lake, his breathing getting heavier, his leg threatening to give way, his pursuer closing on him. Another fence loomed up in front of him. This obviously wasn't a walking area, he thought grimly. He stared at the dark water, removed his fleece and his shoes and waded in to the lake which shelved surprisingly quickly. The coldness of the water took his breath away but he struck out for the far shore. His pursuer stood at the water's edge and cursed.

Twenty-Two

A friend had recommended the Café Comte de Flandre and Hendrickx liked its air of informality. He scribbled a series of calculations in his notepad and sat back, satisfied with the results. He removed his keys and his phone from his pocket and placed them carefully on the table, to the left of the notepad. A tray holding an espresso and a brandy appeared by his shoulder and the drinks were deposited to the right of his notepad. He watched through the window as the drizzle fell steadily on a sea of umbrellas, the sombre black mixing with the frivolous pinks and purples, the pointy ears and the frilly fringes.

Out of the corner of his eye Hendrickx saw a man approach his table. The man asked him if he minded sharing it. The café was busy with mid-morning coffee drinkers and he waved his hand to indicate that the seat was free. The man kept checking his watch and then pulled a laptop from his rucksack. He concentrated on the small machine, barely stopping to sip his cappuccino. Hendrickx ordered another brandy and reached in his briefcase for his newspaper. He checked the stock market reports and ringed a couple of recommended buys. He was surprised when the man sitting opposite started speaking to him.

"I'm sorry to bother you, but I wonder if you could take a look at this. I've left my glasses behind and I can't read this name." He turned his laptop so that Hendrickx could see the screen and then stood up and moved around the table himself. "If you could tell me what you think is written there …"

Hendrickx was annoyed that his peace and quiet had been interrupted in this way. He sighed and reached into his inside jacket pocket for his spectacle case. He stared at the grainy picture on the screen, taking a while to focus properly. It was a shot of a boat and the name on the hull was clearly visible – the *Argent*. Hendrickx continued to stare at the screen, not knowing how to react.

"Is this some sort of joke, young man? Who are you and what is this all about?"

The young man pressed a key on the laptop to start a video clip and Hendrickx watched a group of women bobbing up and down on the sea, in the dark, in a rubber dinghy. Hendrickx started to reach for his keys and his phone, but stopped abruptly when the man began to read a list of names out loud. Hendrickx rose from his chair and glanced nervously around the café, but nobody was paying the two of them any attention. The place was full of noisy conversation.

"Why don't you sit down, Mr Hendrickx, and we can talk. I've got a story to tell you and it may take a little while."

Ryck wasn't sure how he managed to keep his voice steady, but he knew his legs would have given way, had he not immediately sat down. He told Hendrickx about his evening on the *Leopold*, about the dancing, the women clambering aboard, cold, tired and frightened, about the visit paid by the customs officers and about the women being driven away in the Renault. By the time Ryck had finished, Hendrickx had regained his composure and glared across the table.

"That's been very entertaining young man, but you're wasting my time. Now if you don't mind, I have an appointment." He started to rise from his seat once again, but found he was being pushed back into it by someone from behind.

"I think it would be premature for you to leave, Mr Hendrickx! I mean we haven't been formally introduced yet."

"I was wondering when you'd turn up, Harry, where have you been?" Ryck moved his rucksack off the third chair and Vos sat down. He ignored his nephew's question and pulled a camera from a supermarket plastic bag.

"Here, I've got some pictures for you, Hendrickx."

"Christ, not you too! I've already told this idiot that this has nothing to do with me. I'm leaving now and I'd advise you not to get in my way."

"If you leave now," Ryck said, "we'll just have to hand our film shows over to the police."

"There's absolutely nothing linking me to any of this," Hendrickx said, his contempt obvious.

"I wouldn't be too sure about that," Vos cut in. "Firstly we have some very interesting information provided by a lawyer friend of ours. Secondly we have a tape of a phone call which I would describe as incriminating and thirdly we have this snap of you." Vos held his camera up in front of Hendrickx. "A good likeness, don't you think? I would have thought you'd have more sense than to turn up at the delivery point, but obviously you just couldn't stay away. Still, it's up to you, Mr Hendrickx. You are of course free to leave – unlike the women you've been trafficking. The police will no doubt catch up with you sooner or later." Vos reached for his handkerchief and blew his nose. "And I wouldn't fancy your chances after we've spoken to the Group. After all, they have their reputation to think about."

Hendrickx looked at Vos for a long while before speaking.

"Of course – Harry – I knew the name rang a bell. You're the one who's screwing the lovely Katerine, aren't you? I might have guessed she wouldn't keep her part of the deal. I've already paid you off and now you're back for more."

"Katerine has got nothing to do with this. But you're right, we

are after money. In fact we have a list of demands. Once you agree
to them and pay up, you'll be free to go on your way."

Hendrickx's aggression drained away.

"Look, I need some time to think about all this. We can't have
a proper conversation here – it's too public. Why don't we go..."
Vos interrupted him.

"We'll leave when we're ready, Hendrickx, the three of us
together and we'll be going to wherever you keep your piggybank."
Vos reached across the table and grabbed Hendrickx's phone.
"Just a precaution you understand, in case you were tempted to
call for back up. Now, why don't we order some more drinks and
something to eat? I don't know about you two, but I'm starving."

Twenty-Three

Vos and Ryck took the N1 to Mechelen on the way back to Heist.

"So why didn't the guy jump in the water and swim after you?" Despite his lack of sleep, Ryck was keen to know the details of his uncle's late night adventures.

"Well I can only assume that he couldn't swim. Either that or he didn't want to get his suit wet. Standing on the far side of the lake, soaked through, dripping water, and shoeless, I hadn't a clue what to do next. But my decision was almost made for me. I saw this police car cruising down the road and I flagged it down without really thinking. I told them I'd been mugged and had jumped in the lake to escape. They clearly didn't believe my story for a minute so they took me to the station and put me in a cell – again! They played at interrogating me but eventually they must have concluded that I was either completely harmless or round the bend. Anyway they decided to let me go. Very kindly, they gave me a pair of shoes." Ryck looked puzzled.

"Wait a minute. What about the camera? How did you stop the cops from getting hold of it?"

"Just before they picked me up I slung it and the car keys in the bushes by the lake shore. I was pretty certain the camera would be OK there, at least until morning and I wasn't bothered about the keys. Once I'd been released, it took me a while to get back to the lakeside. Then I had to find a bus – two buses in fact to get me back to J's. Luckily I had enough money in coins to pay the fare – my notes were sopping wet and I couldn't find a taxi that would take a card."

"Presumably your phone was out of action after your little swim."

"Completely useless and once the cops had let me go, I couldn't find a public phone that was working either, so I couldn't let you know what had happened. When I eventually got to J's, he told me where you and Hendrickx would be. His friend Kip did a great job, tracking Hendrickx all night and into the morning. I have to say it was a good choice of café!"

"And what about the car?"

"When I called Rodenbach on J's phone and told him I'd had to abandon his car, he actually laughed. I hadn't realised he was capable of laughter. He said he'd stolen the Ford in the first place, so he wasn't at all bothered. I couldn't believe it. There was me driving around in a stolen car half the night. More importantly I asked him about the camera. I was pretty certain it was waterproof, but it was a relief to get it confirmed." They drove in silence for a while.

"We make a good team, Ryck – thanks. Where do you want dropping off?"

"Oh – at the station. Let's hope the Vespa's still where I left it!"

+ + +

As Vos opened his front door he heard the landline ringing. He didn't recognise the caller's number but, as soon as he picked up the phone, he recognised the rasping voice. It sounded like the man had one of those inserts in his neck. Vos couldn't remember what they were called.

"I'm just checking that you're going to turn up tonight, Mr Vos." Vos had actually forgotten all about his appointment with the caller.

"Of course! I made the appointment, didn't I?" The man muttered something inaudible. "Why don't you give me an idea of what this is all about?" Vos asked. The man sounded reluctant at first.

"Very well then. It's about my father. He's recently gone into a home. He's in a wheelchair and starting to get really forgetful. Anyway, I visited the other day and took him some of his things I'd collected from the bungalow. He told me in a very quiet voice that he wanted his gun. I nearly fell off the chair. And then I remembered, he'd showed me a gun once, long, long ago. I must have been about ten. I told him he couldn't take a gun into a care home, but he wanted me to check that it was still there in its hidey-hole – under the floorboards in the bedroom, would you believe? He wanted his diary as well, one he'd kept during the war. He always maintained he was in the resistance but I've had my suspicions about that."

Vos wondered where all this was going. It had been an extremely long night and he just wanted to get showered, have a coffee and go to bed.

"What do you want me to do?" he asked bluntly.

"I'm coming to that, Mr Vos. When I went back to the bungalow, I knew straight away that someone had been in it. Things had been moved. And that's not all. The gun and the diary were missing. I was shocked, I can tell you. I had a look around in other likely places, but there was no trace of either."

"Does anybody else have a key to the bungalow?" Vos asked wearily.

"Well, that's the problem. I checked with Father and it's more a question of who doesn't have a bloody key. The cleaner has one, the care people haven't handed their key back yet, the neighbour has one just-in-case sort of thing, my brother in law has one and he's an ex-con."

"Well that doesn't mean anything, does it?!" Vos' patience was wearing thin. "I mean, I'm an ex-con." There was silence at the other end of the phone. "But that was years ago, I was only sixteen," he added hurriedly. "So have you gone to the police about this?"

"I can't, can I? The gun's not registered or anything and I can't be certain yet that it's actually missing. And I'm worried about the diary. I think it may contain things which we wouldn't want anyone else to know."

"What kind of things?" Vos asked, becoming more interested.

"Um…you know, things to do with what Father really was up to in the war. He's never let me read the diary and got very angry the only time I ever asked him about it. So what I want you to do is to search the bungalow – you know a fresh pair of eyes always helps and if you can't find the missing items, talk to all the people who have keys. I'll pay good money, that's not a problem."

Vos was not sure he wanted another case quite so quickly. But he was intrigued by the story the man had told him, even if he was long-winded. He told him he'd think about the best way forward and go through the details when they met that evening.

He decided he couldn't wait for the coffee or the shower and fell asleep as soon as he lay down on the bed.

+ + +

Ryck watched as the ducks chased each other to scoop up the pieces of bread he'd thrown into the village pond. He walked across the green and knocked on the door of the nearest bungalow. The old lady recognised him. They sat at an old oak table and, as the kettle boiled, she cut him a slice of chocolate cake.

"I just thought I'd come and see how you are," Ryck said "and to tell you that Barto has settled in well with my uncle Harry. I thought at first my other uncle, Pieter, might have taken him, but once he realised the dog would need walking several times a day, that put paid to the idea. The other thing I wanted to mention was about those CDs – you remember, the ones you gave me." The old lady nodded and reached for her handkerchief. "Simone used two of them to store some vital information which helped us crack the case we've been working on. I just thought you'd like to know." He pushed another piece of cake into his mouth.

"I won't pretend I knew what she was involved in." Mrs Josse's voice was unsteady. "She didn't tell me much – in fact I asked her not to. We didn't agree on a lot of things, mainly to do with politics. I don't know if I should tell you this. I'm sorry I've forgotten your name."

"It's Ryck."

"Ryck – that was my brother's name. Of course he's dead now. But – to get back to my daughter. I hired a lawyer. I wasn't satisfied with what I read in the paper about her death." She stopped to blow her nose. "They said it was her heart. But she never had a problem with her heart, in fact she was as fit as a fiddle. So I got the lawyer to create a stink and now they're going to carry out another autopsy. Part of me just wants it all to go away but I have to find out the truth."

Ryck wondered about the implications of this unexpected news. Did that mean Simone had been killed after all and if so, by whom? Ryck decided he wouldn't tell Harry about the second autopsy. He didn't want his uncle deciding to re-start his investigation. And, surely, it would be up to the police to take the case up.

"I'm very sorry to hear that, Mrs Josse. It must be very difficult for you. I'm sure the police will find out what happened."

"Oh, they'll go through the motions, Ryck, but they don't really like people like Simone. She's just a troublemaker to them. I don't imagine they'll get very far."

Ryck thought he might talk to Jalloh. He'd know what to do.

+ + +

Katerine looked up for inspiration. She wanted to change the way her lecture started, use something that would grab her students' attention from the off. She stared back at the screen, but the words wouldn't come. She knew when she was in this kind of mood that she could waste hours thinking in circles. It didn't make any difference whether she worked in her cramped office at the university, which she shared with a particularly garrulous colleague or, like now, in the solitude of her study at home. Either way, when she dried up she had to call it a day.

The buzz of the intercom announced Jalloh's arrival.

"Yes – come on up, J." She'd always had a soft spot for him, despite the fact that their relationship had never really worked.

She went to the front door of the apartment and opened it, just as Jalloh reached the top step, clearly out of breath.

"You can always use the lift, you know." She hugged him and kissed him on the cheek.

"Yes, I know but my doctor keeps telling me I'm supposed to exercise. Too much weight you know," he said, patting his stomach.

They sat side by side on the living room floor propped up against the sofa, a habit they'd got into during their brief period as a couple.

"So, Katerine, you want the inside story on Hendrickx. What did Harry tell you? Not enough I suppose, otherwise I wouldn't be here!" She nodded. "OK, well you know all about the way Hendrickx operates. I don't like the guy, but I have to say he's been good for the Group, pushing it in directions that they'd never have gone otherwise – and most of them good. But he was undone by his gambling. He needed money quickly, a lot of it, so he took the trafficking on as if it was any another project, except of course he didn't tell anyone."

"How did it all end with the Group?" Katerine reached for another cushion. Her back was aching but she didn't want to move from the floor.

"Not surprisingly, they were appalled. All their painstaking work threatened by Hendrickx and his need for quick cash. They've cut him out of the organisation and destroyed all the incriminating evidence they could find. They know Hendrickx won't talk, because of the dirt they have on him. Rodenbach was the one who blew the whistle so he's cool and dear Simone, bless her, can't say a word. So that just leaves your man and his nephew in the know. I've done my best to persuade the Group that neither of them will talk. After all, Harry and Ryck are complicit up to a point. They've known what's been going on and haven't said a word to the police. Come to think of it, you're in the same boat, Katerine."

"You're right – but I suppose the difference is they've known me for a long time whereas Harry and Ryck are newcomers. And what about the women – the ones brought in on the *Leopold*? Did that turn out as you'd planned?"

"It did, thank God!" Jalloh shifted his position and sat cross-legged, his back erect. "Harry did a good job there screwing the money out of Hendrickx. He got Rodenbach to do the heavy work of negotiating with the pimps to buy the women out of their so-called contracts. I think that part of the job was a bit beyond our Harry. Rodenbach's managed to get work and papers sorted out for them. Sure he's making money out of it, but the women have got what they want as well – up to a point anyway. But enough of that. How's it going to go with you and Harry now?"

Katerine stood up, walked to the window and looked out at the trees which were swaying gently in the breeze. She watched a squirrel in the twilight as, high up, it leapt between two trees and scurried down the trunk to the lawn.

"I'm not sure, J. We seem to have got over the worst bit. When he found out all about the smuggling and my extra-curricular activity he wasn't too happy. Of course he wasn't. But we're still seeing each other so he must have come to terms with it."

She went into the kitchen and put the kettle on. She didn't want to turn the lights on, preferring the evening to creep into the kitchen slowly.

Twenty-Four

There was a clear view out over the becalmed sea. Tiny waves lapped lazily along the shoreline as a pair of seagulls fought over the remains of a discarded sandwich.

Vos had been in two minds as to whether to come back to the beach near De Haan. His recent visits had not left good memories. But he liked the place too much and wanted to exorcise the ghosts. He thought about Moise. He was pleased he and Katerine had been able to deliver the compensation to his family, and hand it over personally.

There'd been about a dozen of them gathered in a tiny single storey house in a village near Kambove. They'd been unable to hear themselves talk whilst the rainstorm lashed down on the corrugated iron roof and stood politely and somewhat awkwardly smiling at each other, waiting for the storm to finish. They'd managed to understand each other using a mixture of French and Katerine's Kingwana. Moise's mother had been devastated by her son's death but she'd put on a brave face and had welcomed them into her home. Word had soon got round the village about the visitors and the money.

Katerine and Vos had realised from the start that there was nothing they could do to control how the money might be used. They'd been particularly wary of one man who'd said he was Moise's uncle. The other family members eyed him with thinly disguised hostility. Vos hoped the mother and adult sons – Moise's brothers – would be strong enough to keep control of the cash.

The brothers had told Vos that, like Moise, they were both miners. They'd been unable to get jobs with the big mining companies and more dangerous work in the small illegal mines was all they could find. They were constantly worried about getting caught or injured in a mining accident. They said Moise had been the brightest in the family and that he had decided to find some other way of spending his life. His journey north had been long and difficult. He'd managed to phone his family a couple of times to tell them what was happening, but then everything had gone quiet and they'd feared the worst.

Barto ran ahead, in and out of the waves. Vos still wasn't sure whether he'd done the right thing taking on the dog, but Ryck had been very persuasive, strangely so for someone who had always been wary of anything canine.

Vos had eventually managed to come to terms with Katerine's work with the Group. He could understand how it might have been possible to get sucked in and to turn a blind eye to the illegality. For a while though he'd felt he'd been used by her, that she should have told him everything from the start. He'd started to see less of her. Much to his surprise, it was his mother of all people who'd told him not to be so stupid. She'd taken an instant liking to Katerine and told him bluntly that his chances of attracting anyone else half as good as her were nil – particularly at his age and in 'his condition' as she'd untactfully, but typically phrased it.

Katerine, barefoot, chased the dog along the shore. The dog barked as she held a large stick high above him before throwing it into the waves. The dog bounded through the water to retrieve the stick. Katerine's phone buzzed. She read the text and then wished she hadn't. "Don't think you've heard the last of me – First Base". She decided to ignore it, confident that she had more on Hendrickx than he had on her – and she certainly wasn't going to mention it to anyone else.

Vos caught up with her and the dog.

"How do you fancy spending a weekend in a pensioner's bungalow?" he asked, squinting into the sun.

"Well you certainly know how to charm a girl – how could I possibly refuse? What on earth will we be doing in this bungalow?"

"Searching for something – a gun actually, but I'm not telling you any more just now." She stared at him.

"And once we've visited the bungalow, how about a trip to London?"

"That's more like it. Are we going to see Kim? I'd like to meet her."

"Yes, she phoned me out of the blue, without any mention of Josina, which I took as a positive sign. I can't promise you'll get on, but let's wait and see."

"I'll look forward to it. Now – tell me more about this gun."

"No – later! We've got a present to give to the man who runs the bar on the other side of these dunes. Let's go."

Katerine ran ahead chased by the dog. Vos followed slowly, his stick flicking through the marram grass, a look of quiet satisfaction on his face.

Acknowledgments

Thanks to Gabrielle, Claire, Tom, Jim, Paul and Emma for their encouragement and support.

By the same author

DARKSTONE

THE **FUTURE** MAY BE **CLOSER** THAN YOU **THINK...**

Ellis Landsman, a forester living in the Scottish Outlands in the 2020's is shocked to find a wolf in his forest uncovering the body of a young woman.

He rescues the body and makes the long snow-covered journey to Glasgow to report the death and hand the body over to the Brigade, the semi-militaristic security force that has replaced the police.

But Ellis doesn't trust the Brigade to investigate the death and decides to try and find out for himself who the woman is, how she died and how she came to be buried on his land.

But all is not as it seems as Ellis struggles to track down the young woman's killer...

214